CONSPIRACY IN THE CAPITOL

B. IVY WOODS

BRETAGEY PRESS

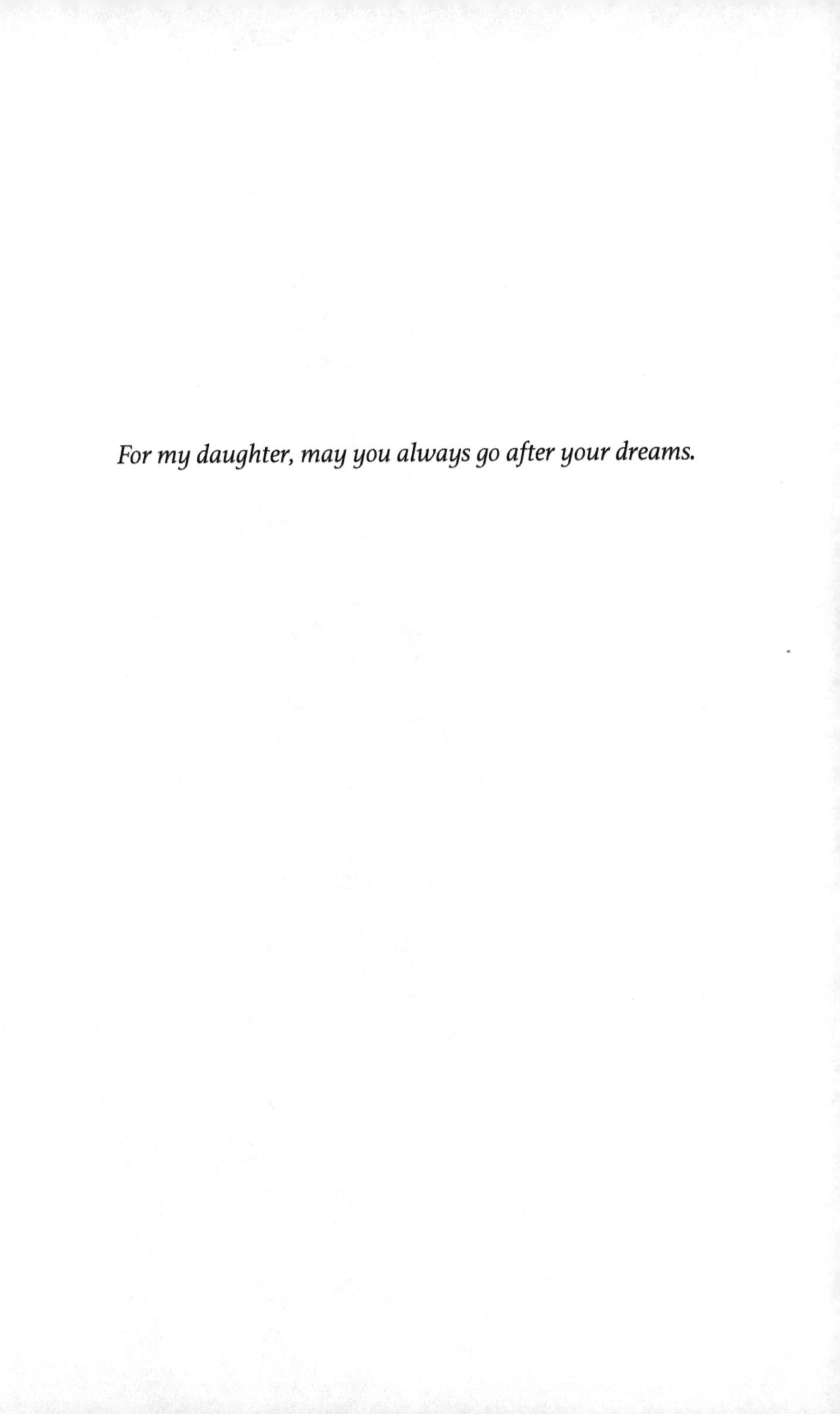

For my daughter, may you always go after your dreams.

1

———

If she walked faster, she just might make it. Could running across the street result in her death? Potentially.

As the seconds decreased on the timer, Rachelle "Rae" Carter turned and fought the urge to burst into a sprint. After all, she had spent too much time getting ready for tonight for it all to be for naught. She knew she could make this light.

Focusing on her stride, Rae darted across the street before the walk sign's hand became steady. She was almost at the other side, but that thought came to a halt when a loud beep startled her just before she reached the sidewalk.

Rae swung around, looking for the offender, and realized the driver was beeping at another car that had pulled out of their parking space and into a busy intersection. She turned around and strolled down the street to a place that she knew all too well. The Green Hat had been her after-work spot for several years now. Rae sidestepped a couple that was exiting the establishment and made her way into the bar. Feeling the immense amount of heat radiating from the room, she took off her jacket that had come in handy while she was out in the cool early fall evening.

"Rae, we're over here!"

Rae turned around and waved at the three women at a table close to the bar. She shoved her way through the crowd to make her way to them. "I'm sorry I'm late!" she exclaimed while pulling out the only chair left at the table. She glanced at the bar and made eye contact with John. John was the owner of The Green Hat, and it had been in his family for decades. He took over ownership a few months before Rae and her friends started coming in for their happy hour. John had taken a liking to them and would often laugh at their funny stories. She waved at John and smiled when he returned the gesture.

"I'm not surprised that I could hear you, Liv, across a crowded bar."

"They don't call me boisterous for nothing." Rae admired Olivia "Liv" Nicholls for her ability to own her labels and use them to her advantage.

"Where have you been?" The question had come from Evelyn "Eve" Jackson, who sent a curious glance Rae's way.

"I got held up at work. My boss pulled me into a meeting at 5:00 p.m., which is a crime in many countries. I'm glad y'all started without me." She placed her coat on the back of her chair and smoothed down the little black dress she'd worn to work. Rae worked as a policy advisor for an environmental nonprofit named Wild Parks, Wild Lands in Arlington, VA. The organization's mission was the protection of public spaces. She had only been there for a few weeks but was enjoying it immensely.

Rae smiled at each woman at the table, and when her

eyes reached Juliana "Jules" Cartwright, the woman held up her drink in solidarity before taking a sip. She and her friends got together biweekly to relax, vent, and to catch up on each other's lives in person.

Rae and Eve met in college. The two met Jules and Liv when they moved back to Washington, DC, at a barre studio they frequented. Their friendship grew over time, and now the women were closer than ever. Being there for one another through the good times, the bad times, the joyous occasions, and the midlife crises—yes, there were multiple—meant that their friendship hadn't wavered and was stronger than ever.

"Do you have any more dating stories to tell us today?" Jules asked Liv. Liv smiled coyly and placed her drink down on the table. Although they had many interests, the one thing that they all could agree on was that dating in the DC area was a nightmare. Liv went out on the most dates by far and the other women usually listened to her adventures.

"Nope. Everything is as dry as a desert on that front. In every sense of the word." Eve rolled her eyes, Rae shook her head, and Jules just stared at Liv after her comment.

Rae picked something to drink off of the menu before flipping it over. "I'm shocked and appalled that you're not holding to your normal standard of several dates in a week, sometimes multiple dates in a day. Is everything all right? Are you sick?" Rae reached over and touched Liv's forehead with the back of her hand before Liv batted her away. The women chuckled before turning their attention back to their drinks.

"How is everything going with y'all? How is work?" Rae took a sip of her water and debated making her way to the bar.

"You know nothing ever stops when it comes to the news.

I'm mentally preparing myself for the election cycle that's about to ramp up." Eve was a reporter for a local DC newspaper that covered local and national politics. This connection kept Rae informed about the ins and outs of politics, which was helpful to her in a personal and professional capacity.

"People love to throw events. Business is not hurting, and I'm so glad that I have coworkers who help share the load. Wedding season is here and is in rare form. I think we have eleven weddings over the next week?" Liv was an event planner for The Kennedy in Georgetown. She had missed some of their last few happy hours because of having to help when her coworkers were out for personal reasons.

"Fundraisers are the name of the game around here." Jules worked for her family's foundation as a manager of marketing and communications. She also sometimes attended events on behalf of the foundation.

"We need to get away. Did we ever decide when we're going to Bermuda?" Rae asked. Eve fist-bumped Rae at the mention of the trip. Liv had brought up going on vacation and the women had wholeheartedly agreed that it was a good idea.

"Finding a time when we're all free might be a challenge," said Liv. She picked up her phone and scrolled through her calendar.

Rae nodded. She pulled her phone out and did the same. "I'm free after this month. We're preparing for our midyear board meeting, and everyone is scrambling to get things together."

"That's understandable," said Jules. She cast a hesitant

glance at Rae twice, both of which Eve caught. Eve raised an eyebrow, while Jules shook her head.

"And now that I'm looking over my schedule, why did I decide to move this month?"

"Rae, I said you were crazy for deciding to move this month, given what time of year it is. This might be the craziest thing you've done in all the years we've known each other." Eve glanced at Rae before grabbing her beer.

"I know, I know. But the perfect apartment came on the market, and it would have been silly to pass it up." Rae was preparing to move into a new apartment in Arlington in a few weeks to be closer to her job and her parents. "Although it isn't the smartest thing I've ever done, I'm riding the wave." Eve rolled her eyes before she smiled at Rae. She always told the girls that they should "ride the wave" whenever they were hesitant to take a chance on something they deep down wanted to do.

Rae cleared her throat. "How's dating going for everyone else? I think we got sidetracked by Liv's answer earlier."

There was an audible groan from both Eve and Jules.

"Don't even ask." Eve gulped down the rest of her beer.

Liv had just drained the rest of her rum and coke before she stood up. "I'm going to head up to the bar to get another. Do you want your usual? Eve, do you want another beer? Jules, anything else?" Both Eve and Rae nodded their heads as Jules shook hers. And with that, Liv was on her way.

The girls were silent as they waited for Liv to return. Rae studied an email on her phone before looking back up. She noticed that Eve was staring at Jules, and Jules was doing everything she could to avoid Eve's gaze.

"Why are you staring at Jules?" Rae asked Eve.

"I think she might have something to tell us." Eve raised her eyebrow again at Jules, receiving a sigh in return.

"I'll wait until Liv gets back," Jules said as she played with her hands. Rae could feel the nervous energy bouncing off of her and was wondering how long she'd been keeping whatever she wanted to tell the group to herself.

"I'm here," Liv announced. She handed Rae her red wine and Eve her beer before she sat down in her seat. Rae took a long sip from her glass and sighed as the liquid went down her throat.

"So, you know how I attended a fundraiser with my dad because my mom couldn't make it last night?" Everyone nodded, remembering the text conversation they'd had about it. "Well, you'll never guess who I ran into." Jules reached over to grab her blond hair, which was draped over her shoulders and played with the ends for a few seconds before folding her hands in her lap.

"The President of the United States?" Liv smirked. Eve laughed, and Rae smiled in response.

"Nope, but I'm not sure that would have been more exciting. I saw Flint West."

The whole table was silent. Jules looked down at her hands, while Eve and Liv stared at her.

Rae's face was blank, but her mouth was agape, revealing how she felt about the news. *Was Flint back in town? Since when?* She swallowed hard before speaking. "You saw Flint? How is he?"

The thought of him still made her heart race and she couldn't decide if she liked that or not. The last time she and Flint had spoken to each other had been cordial, but the couple of months that had led up to them ending their relationship had been tense. But when they were good, everything was fantastic. That included them being long-distance for most of their relationship. The plans they'd made, the dreams they'd shared had gone away several years ago, but sometimes Rae would think about him and wonder what could have been.

"He looked well. He asked about you."

"That's great." Rae made sure that her expression remained unchanged. She took another long sip from her drink. She wouldn't go down that road again.

"What did he ask about her?" Eve asked, turning her attention to Jules. Unsurprisingly, Eve was the one to follow up with a list of questions.

"Well, we didn't have much time to talk because we saw each other just before the speeches began. He asked how Rae was doing and if she still lived in the area." Rae showed no emotion when Jules said her name.

"Interesting." Eve leaned back in her chair and thought for a second. "I didn't realize Flint was back in town."

"He's been back for a few months. His law firm transferred him to the DC area. He lives in Arlington too."

He would. Arlington was a nice size, but it wasn't that big. The probability of them running into each other was high. The thought of that made her nauseous. Their breakup wasn't the cleanest, but it had been for the best at that point in their lives. She hadn't even given much thought to the idea that she might run into his parents too.

"That's good for him. It sounds like he's doing well for himself."

Jules mumbled a reply that no one at the table could catch.

"What was that, Jules?" Liv leaned in closer.

"I said he asked if Rae's phone number was still the same."

Liv turned to face Jules, and her eyes darted from Jules to Rae and back. "He asked if Rae's phone number changed? You have to be kidding. Did he say anything about trying to contact her?"

Jules shook her head and Rae let out a deep breath as she glanced down at her own hands. She could feel someone's eyes on her, and when she looked up, her gaze connected with Eve's.

"I was a little worried about telling you, but I knew you had to know."

Rae's emotional state after the breakup had been rough for weeks. She wasn't surprised that Jules debated telling her because she had seen the toll the breakup had taken on her. Her friends were there to help her pick up the pieces. Rae knew how lucky she was to have their friendship.

"Don't worry about it. Thanks for telling me." Rae downed the rest of her wine before placing the glass back down on the table. She knew that she finished her drink too fast, but she didn't care. She looked around and noticed that Jules was close to finishing hers, too. "Do you guys want something else? I'm paying."

Jules nodded, and Rae stood up from her seat. She felt every bit of that wine when she stood up. Every step toward the bar helped her shake off the thoughts and feelings that came flowing back after the news about Flint. She ordered the drinks and was waiting for them. Rae was thankful that John was busy with a customer and couldn't make their drinks because she didn't want to be friendly or polite. The longer she stood there waiting, the more tension she felt in her temples. Cursing herself for getting worked up enough to cause a headache, she paid for her order, pocketed her credit card, and carried the drinks back to the table.

The conversation had changed since she'd left, and for that, she was grateful. About an hour later, the women finished their drinks, paid any tabs they had opened, and left the bar. Satisfied that the happy hour ended somewhat quickly, Rae sat in the back of a taxi, rubbing her temples. She checked her phone and saw she had no new messages or any notifications and that helped relieve some of the tension that had formed in her head. When she opened her front door, she shook her head and walked to the bathroom. The only thing she wanted to do for the rest of the night was to grab a quick dinner, take a shower, and go to bed.

She took some leftovers from her fridge, placed them in the microwave, and started loading dishes into the dishwasher as she waited for the food to warm up. Once the microwave beeped, she let the food cool down a bit while she finished up her task. When she finished, she scarfed down her food, placed those dishes into the dishwasher, too, started the dishwasher, and headed to her bedroom. Rae texted her girlfriends to let them know she was home and began her bedtime routine.

When she finished up and wandered into her bedroom, her eyes lingered on her laptop. Fighting the urge, Rae gave in and powered it on. There she pulled up her photos application and found photos from five years ago, pictures that she and Flint had taken together. Some images that had been for his eyes only and he had returned the favor.

Rae knew of a way she could get rid of the tension that

involved rummaging into her bedside table, but denied herself that right. Getting annoyed with herself for even digging up those old photos, she closed the laptop, grabbed her phone, and wandered over to her bed. Putting her phone on do not disturb, she placed it next to her on her bed and passed out.

"Did you find anything in that rack?"

Rae turned around to face Jules and shook her head. The two were out shopping for clothes on a beautiful early fall afternoon. Rae knew the heat would come back for a second round, but was taking advantage of a cool day in the DC area. The women had already found a couple of things, but they had not accomplished their main goal of picking up a few professional outfits for work on sale.

Leaving the store in a huff, Rae and Jules strolled past more stores before deciding they should take a break to eat. They settled on a seafood restaurant, and while they were waiting for their food, Jules's phone rang.

"I wonder who this is," muttered Jules as she picked up the phone. Rae tried not to pay attention to the conversation, but the tide changed when Jules looked at her wide-eyed.

"What's up?" whispered Rae. Jules motioned for her to give her a second as she returned her attention to the conversation. Her curiosity piqued, Rae tried to control her annoyance due to her lack of patience. It was something she was working on, but she threw her efforts out the window in her present state. Was this conversation about her? If so, why?

Rae couldn't help tapping her fingers on the table while she waited for Jules to wrap up her call. The waiter returned with their food and set the plates in front of them.

"Hey, Mom. Our food just arrived, can I call you later?"

Jules's mom mentioned something about her? Mrs. Cartwright was a lovely woman, but she and Rae didn't interact. Maybe this had nothing to do with her. Rae thought for a second and had an aha moment. Flint. It might be about him.

Jules ended the call, and it took everything for Rae not to ask Jules a million and a half questions. "So?"

"My mom said hello, and she hoped you were doing well. I need to pick up her favorite perfume because she is running low, and my dad forgot to order it."

Rae side-eyed her. "That couldn't have been what made you stare at me like a deer in headlights when you were talking to her."

"She mentioned something exciting about Flint."

Rae swallowed hard. "And what's that?" She didn't know if she wanted to hear the answer to this question. She couldn't lie to herself. She did.

"A local magazine featured him and released it today."

The nervousness oozed out of Rae's body. That wasn't so bad. "Congrats to him. He should have sat down for an interview with Eve instead."

Jules nodded before saying, "There were a few tidbits that were...interesting, to say the least."

"Are you going to keep dragging this out, or are you going to tell me what's going on? Does this have anything to do with me?"

"My mom is sending me a copy of the article, so I'll show it to you in a minute. I don't want to dive into anything until we have the article, but it was nothing bad as far as I heard." And that sent Rae's heart into overdrive. She was thankful that the tablecloth covered her bouncing foot.

Rae and Jules ate in silence until a ping came from Jules's phone. She picked it up, hit a few keys, and smiled.

"Here you go," she said as she flipped the phone around for Rae to see. The photo of Flint was stunning. The proper words to describe it were *sexy* and *sophisticated*. He was wearing a black suit that fit him like a glove, a white button-down shirt, and a blue tie. Rae could see hints of the man she knew when they dated several years ago, but the differences surprised her. Gone were the Air Force uniform and in its place was a beautifully tailored suit that fit him perfectly. She started reading the article and grinned as she read his accomplishments in the Air Force and his life afterward. The journalist wrote the article in a question-and-answer format, which made it easy to find Flint's quotes.

"He cofounded a foundation to help combat homelessness in the veteran community? And in part funded it?" Rae asked, looking up at Jules.

"Yes. I think Flint hit it big by investing in a company that went public. The Wests' fortune is also nothing to sneeze at. We've given donations to the foundation in the past."

"Why didn't you mention it to me before?"

Jules sighed and looked down at her hands before looking back at Rae. "I wasn't at liberty to mention what organizations we donate or provide grants. Plus, he kept his involvement with the organization on the down-low until it leaked about a month ago."

Rae did a double-take. "First, since when do you say down-low? Second, I'm not shocked Flint co-founded this organization, because he always talked about how he wanted to help others. I didn't expect he would do it in this capacity."

"What's wrong with saying down-low? Anyway, now that everyone knows he cofounded this organization with a friend, it will probably lead to a lot more exposure for veteran homelessness, the foundation, and him. That wasn't the only thing I wanted you to see. Keep reading."

Rae did just that. She resisted the urge to skim, which came naturally to her when reading longer items. She continued her quest to find the other part of the article that Jules wanted her to read.

"What the hell?!" screamed Rae. She didn't realize she'd screamed and jumped out of her seat until she surveyed the restaurant. The patrons that were quietly enjoying their meals and drinks around their table were now staring at her. When she looked down and realized she was standing, Rae apologized and slinked back down into her seat. Shuffling her chair closer to the table, she put her elbows on the table and her head in her hands. She then rubbed her eyes and grabbed the phone again. Rae moved it closer to her face to reread the line again and again. She couldn't be reading these words.

The interviewer asked him about his love life as a throwaway question near the end of the profile.

Question: Is one of Northern Virginia's most eligible bachelors still single or is there someone special in your life?

Answer: I am single because I let "the one" get away years ago. When I came to my senses, she had already moved on to bigger and better things. If I had the opportunity to date her again, I would do it in a heartbeat.

"You know he's talking about you, right?"

"We don't know that for sure." What she did know was that line had removed any appetite she had left for the rest of her shrimp and grits.

"But your mind jumped to the same conclusion mine did."

Rae didn't confirm Jules's comment, but she was right. The interviewer gushed over his answer before ending the article.

"Well, that was...something." Rae's thoughts were jumbled. She stopped the bouncing of her leg by shifting her position in the seat.

"I knew he was still interested in you."

"We don't know if he's talking about me. Who knows how many people he might have been in relationships with over the years."

"True. But based on the article, it sounds like the woman he was with before a lot of his more recent accomplishments. Like he might have still been in the service."

Rae shrugged. "Who knows? They could have taken his comments out of context." Jules wiggled her eyebrows at her and that was when Rae knew that Jules had spent too much time hanging out with Liv. "Are you going to ask him?"

Jules laughed out loud. "Probably not, but you could if you wanted to."

"Are you crazy? I haven't spoken to him in years. I don't even know if his number is still the same."

"Doesn't mean you can't speak to him now. You're on his brain. And now I'm convinced that he is on yours." Jules paused before opening and closing her mouth. She opened her mouth once more and said, "Hell, he also knows that your number hasn't changed, so maybe he will reach out."

Rae rolled her eyes and gave up. Jules wouldn't let her win this, so there was no point in arguing about it.

"I found it interesting that the interviewer seemed to push the idea that he might run for Congress someday. Scratch that. The interviewer was urging him to consider running, and he brushed it off." Rae thanked herself for her quick thinking and coming up with a reason to change the subject.

"I thought that was interesting too. I know Flint lives in Arlington, and I haven't heard anything about Rep. John Clarkson retiring, so I am not even sure where that came from."

"Maybe it's just a thought for the future since he has plenty of time to run."

Rae shrugged, but Flint potentially running for Congress rolled around in her head. Based on what she read in that article, he sounded like a strong candidate to run for office. Being young, smart, and having served his country and continuing to help would all be points in his favor. It didn't hurt that he was well-spoken and attractive. And that thought caused Rae to snap out of the mini daydream she was having about Flint.

"Are you almost finished? And did you still want to check to see if we could find your mother's perfume?" Rae drank from the glass of water in front of her before placing it back on the table. She took her hair out of the ponytail and let it drape around her shoulders.

Jules nodded as she patted her lips with her napkin. Rae chuckled at the expressions Jules was making as she tried to remove any remains of the salad she had been eating without ruining her lipstick.

"You know you could just reapply it, right?"

The "no shit, Sherlock" look on Jules's face made Rae chuckle again. She pulled out her credit card in anticipation of the bill while Jules was finishing refreshing her makeup, their waiter returned. Rae slapped her hand over the receipt and handed it and her credit card to the waiter so Jules wouldn't have a chance to grab her wallet.

"Didn't you pay for our drinks last week at happy hour? Plus, you drove us here. I got this."

Jules beamed. "Thanks, lady."

Once they settled the check, the two strolled around the shopping area to see if anything else looked appealing.

"Can we stop in this store? I know they have a decent perfume selection, so maybe the brand my mom uses is here."

Rae nodded as the two entered the department store. Thankfully, Mrs. Cartwright's perfume was in stock, so Jules grabbed the one she wanted and took it to the register.

"There is one thing I forgot to ask you," Jules mentioned as they were sitting in Jules's car on the way back to Arlington. The two had spent another hour at the stores before calling it quits. Their shopping trip was somewhat successful, so Rae couldn't complain.

"What would you do if you saw Flint again? Chances are it will happen since we all live close to each other."

"Wait, what do you mean we all live close to each other?" Rae's glare could melt steel. What else was Jules keeping from her?

"Um, yeah. I told you Flint lives in Arlington."

"Arlington isn't small."

"Oops. Well, he doesn't live too far from us." Rae had found an apartment that was a few blocks away from Jules's building.

"Where does he live, Jules?" As soon as the words left her mouth, she realized her tone sounded harsh. "Sorry, I didn't mean to say it like that."

"No worries. And I'm sorry I didn't tell you. I swore I did. Anyway, he isn't too far from the Ballston Metro. I'm not sure exactly where."

Rae did a double-take. "Oh, you meant literally in my soon-to-be future neighborhood."

Jules cringed. "I swore I told you."

"Don't worry about it. I'm not changing my moving plans for him. If we run into each other, I'll act like a perfectly normal, rational adult." Rae paused. "I'll hit him over the head with a frying pan."

Jules snorted and glanced at her friend. "I'm sure that will go over well. You wouldn't want to ruin the face of one of Arlington's most eligible bachelors."

"No. We couldn't have that, could we?"

3

____

A few days later, Rae checked her calendar on her work laptop and saw that she had enough time to get lunch and bring it back to her desk. She knew she had to continue working while she ate, but also knew getting some fresh air would do her good. Delighted at the idea of taking a break from looking at the slides she had been working on for the better part of the day, she slid her black blazer over her dress, grabbed her purse, and walked downstairs.

Rae was thankful that her office was near one of the food truck gathering areas, which would hopefully cut down on the time she would be away from her desk. She quickly ordered two tacos at one of the many food trucks, paid for the order, and stepped aside to wait. She checked her phone to see if there were any emails, and when she glanced up, her heart ended up in her throat.

She thought she saw someone she once knew.

"Flint?" she whispered. Rae tried to get a look at the man walking across the street with his back to her. Before she could think about it further, they called her order up. Snatching the food off the truck counter, she headed back to her office.

Rae was about to dig into her food when her office phone rang. Danielle, her boss, called Rae to give her the answers she needed ahead of Danielle walking into her next meeting. Rae breathed a sigh of relief and turned her attention back to her tacos. Just as she was about to finish the last taco, some salsa landed on her upper thigh. To make matters worse, Rae had chosen a beige cocktail dress to wear to work today, so the stain was visible.

Rae growled at the stain. "This would happen to me," she muttered as she grabbed a napkin and tried to get the spot out. When that did nothing, she jumped up, banging her knee on the desk.

"Ow," howled Rae as she rubbed the spot where her knee met the desk. Could her luck get any worse? She grabbed her cell phone and hobbled over to her door. She switched to the flats she always kept in her office and swung the door open impatiently. She rushed down the hall so fast that her coworkers might have mistaken her for Allyson Felix. Days like today, she wished her office was closer to the bathroom. Rae stood in the bathroom and did everything she could to get the stain out. Although it was less noticeable, she could still see it, but she hoped that was because she was looking for it. Deciding that the answer to her problem would be to throw on the black blazer that she kept at her office in case she needed to run to Capitol Hill for a meeting, she breathed a small sigh of relief. She washed her hands, grabbed her phone, and started the long journey back to her desk on the other side of the office. Thankfully, her knee had stopped throbbing, so at least she had that going for her.

Rae was on her phone checking her email when she briefly glanced up as she walked past the glass windowpanes of the main conference room. Suddenly she stopped in her tracks. That couldn't be who she thought it was.

Flint. In her office. Right now. In the conference room with Danielle, Danielle's boss, and the CEO.

Rae's mouth flew open. She knew staring was rude, but she couldn't help herself. Her boss, Danielle, looked up and raised an eyebrow at her. That motion was enough to snap Rae out of whatever daze she was in and to propel her feet forward. She turned her head, doing her best to focus on the path in front of her, but she could see Flint had looked up. She turned to her left, and his eyes caught hers. But Rae was better prepared after getting caught staring by her boss. She hurriedly walked past the conference room and was thankful that her office was on the other side of the building. If he wanted to come and find her, he would have to hunt her down.

When she reached her office, she caught herself on the door as she almost slammed it in her excitement at getting through that noninteraction unscathed. Rae pulled out her phone and hammered a text to her friends.

Rae: SOS.

She hoped someone would respond quickly, but given that it was the middle of the workday, that was up in the air. As she waited, she wiped the mist of sweat she hadn't realized had formed off of her forehead. Whether it was from seeing Flint or practically sprinting to her office, she didn't know.

The sudden vibration of her phone caused her to jump out of her seat.

Jules: Everything okay?

Rae: No. You wouldn't believe who is in my office right now.

Eve: Who could it possibly be that would make you this jumpy?

Rae wasn't surprised that Eve could read her mood even over a text message.

Rae: Flint.

Jules: Shut the front door!

Liv: What she meant was shut the fuck up. Do you know why he's there? Did you talk to him? Please tell me you didn't freak out.

Rae: No freak-outs because he was several feet away in a conference room surrounded by a bunch of people and my boss. No idea why he's here, and thankfully I didn't have an opportunity to talk to him. And now I'm wondering if I can play sick and get out of here.

Eve: You wouldn't want to leave when he's leaving. Do you know what time that meeting is ending?

Rae silently thanked Eve for her voice of reason as she scrolled through her boss's calendar to see when the meeting was ending.

Rae: Looks like it's ending in 10 minutes. I can get out of here in 3.

Eve: And what if the meeting ends early?

And just like that, Rae wanted Eve's "voice of reason" to eat shit.

Rae: I guess I need to hunker down in my office.

Liv: Aye aye, matey! Jules, did you tell Flint anything about where Rae worked when you saw him recently?

Jules: Nope. He asked what she was up to, but I didn't name specifics. It probably wouldn't be hard to find out information on her, though. All it would take was a simple search online.

Rae sighed as she threw her head back and reclined in her chair. What was she going to do?

Rae: *Maybe he won't come this way. I assume the big bosses called the meeting with his firm, not the other way around.*

Liv: *I highly doubt it. Based on the article Jules sent us, fat chance of that.*

Jules: *Yeah...I don't know if his visiting your office was a complete coincidence.*

Rae: *Jules, I can't remember if you mentioned where he worked last night. Do you know?*

She knew damn well Jules hadn't mentioned where he was working last night.

Jules: *Sure, it's for the same firm that his father owns. It doesn't mean he doesn't do consulting on the side. But I'd lean more toward it being firm-related.*

Why would Wild Parks, Wild Lands be hiring another law firm outside of the lawyers they already used? And what did it have to do with Danielle? The buzzing of her phone snapped her out of the rabbit hole her thoughts were about to go down.

Liv: *I think he knew you worked there. I don't believe in coincidences.*

Rae didn't either, if she had to be honest. She took a deep breath to calm her racing heart. She was a grown who could handle this.

Rae: *What type of law did you say he practiced, Jules?*

Rae knew Jules had never mentioned what type of law he practiced either.

Jules: *Corporate law? Tax law? I'm not sure.*

As she was composing a response, there was a knock on her door. She briefly glanced at the clock on her desktop and saw that it was 2:05 p.m. The meeting had definitely ended.

"Come in," she said as she took in a deep breath.

Her breath whooshed out quickly when Danielle poked her head into the room.

"Can we have a quick chat in about fifteen minutes? I need to fill you in on a project I want you to work on."

"Sure. That shouldn't be a problem."

"Great." Danielle paused before continuing, "Are you feeling okay?"

Rae's eyes darted to the left before focusing back on her boss. "Yeah. Why wouldn't I be?"

"You looked startled earlier when you walked past the conference room."

"I saw something strange, that's all." *Well, that wasn't a lie.*

"Okay. I'll meet you back here in fifteen, and then we can chat." Danielle softly closed Rae's office door. Rae closed her eyes before sitting up. She was happy Danielle didn't push any further and got back to work.

Rae checked her email and the second knock on her door made her roll her eyes. With a huff, she glanced at the clock and saw that it was 2:14 p.m.

"Come in!" Rae said. Danielle must have wrapped up whatever she needed to do earlier than planned.

But that would be too much to hope for, because it wasn't Danielle standing in the doorway.

"Hey."

Rae's mouth fell open for the second time that day. She could think of a million things she wanted to say in that exact moment, but her mouth wasn't computing with her brain.

Since she couldn't form the words, she examined him instead. How had he changed in the years since she'd seen him? He had grown out his brown hair. It was still short on the sides but the top of it was longer and was swept back off of his forehead in a coif hairstyle. Her eyes skimmed down his face and body as she mentally made notes of the differences and similarities compared to the last time she'd seen him. He looked to be even stronger than he was when he was in the Air Force. Rae had never seen him in a suit in person before today, and just like how she thought years ago he was made to wear his military uniforms, his body was made to wear suits as well.

There were a lot of things that were the same. The level of intensity and confidence that he manifested when he entered a room had not changed. Neither had the hard angles of his jaw or his crystal-clear blue eyes. And he had those same blue eyes trained on her.

"What the hell are you doing here?"

4

———————

"Wasn't expecting that greeting."

Rae swallowed before saying, "My bad. Let's rewind that." She cleared her throat. "Hey."

Rae smiled because she sounded confident, but deep down, she wasn't. She averted her eyes, but she could still feel his stare.

"How's everything going?" She was glad he was keeping it polite and neutral.

Although he'd asked her a basic question, Rae could feel a rush of feelings coming back to her. Feelings she thought she'd buried over the years were now hitting her like a ton of bricks. Those feelings were attempting to take over her thoughts, but she did her best to keep them at bay so they wouldn't cloud her judgment.

"Not too bad. Super busy, but busy is good. How about yourself?"

"Can't complain, especially right now. You look great, Rae."

The wistfulness in his voice, the rich timbre she had fallen in love with years ago, led her to think about his featured article. If he was talking about their relationship, he was probably thinking back on the good times they'd had, not that she could blame him. But she couldn't stop herself from running through the bad times. It felt as if a bucket of cold water had been dumped on her when she thought about the events leading up to their breakup.

"Um. Thank you. What are you doing here?" Her words might have come out a little more curt than she'd intended, but she wanted him to get right to the chase.

Flint didn't have time to answer because Danielle appeared behind him.

"Excuse me," she said as she scooted past Flint. "Oh good, you've met. Rae, Flint is working on a few things for WPWL, mostly about administrative tasks like governing documents, risk management, etc. If he needs anything, please get it for him. It might help if you guys had a meeting at some point."

Couldn't someone else help him? Plus, she had to prepare for the board meeting and find time to move. Why did she need to meet with him? Why couldn't the floor turn into quicksand and swallow her whole right now?

"Sounds like a great idea." Rae forced another smile on her face.

Danielle turned to Flint and said, "I'll cc you two on an email with what we are envisioning. That way, you'll have a way to contact one another."

Rae wanted to say that he already had her phone number anyway but bit her tongue. Flint glanced at Danielle before his eyes returned to Rae. "Sounds like a plan."

"It was nice meeting you, Mr. West."

"Likewise. I look forward to working with both you and Ms. Carter."

The only time that Flint had called her Ms. Carter was when he joked about her taking his last name when they got married. When. They. Got. Married.

Rae gripped the edge of her desk until the pressure hurt her fingertips. It was the only thing that was keeping her from saying something that she would regret in front of her boss.

"Great. Rae, are you ready?" Danielle headed down the hall before she could finish the question.

As she nodded and stood up, Rae grabbed her phone and her laptop and walked to the door. She changed into her three-inch heels, all the while staring Flint down. Rae was thankful for the burst of confidence that came as she put the heels on. Unless his thoughts had changed, he loved when she wore heels. And by the look in his eye—one he had given her many times before—she could tell that was the only thing he wished she were wearing.

Flint put his hand out to motion for her to pass, and she strutted past him. She was thankful that today was a day she dressed up. A beige dress and nude heels replaced her usual business casual outfit that included a pair of dark skinny jeans, a nice blouse, a dark blazer, and flats. She had worn her long wavy dark brown hair down today on a whim. As she was walking out the door this morning, she'd grabbed a few pieces of gold jewelry that she thought would look good with her outfit and black tote. She knew she looked fantastic, and he could eat his heart out.

"I look forward to working with you, Ms. Carter." His tone and the emphasis on her last name reminded her of the voice he used during foreplay, and it made her quiver. It reeked confidence that went along with the smirk he was sporting. But she was having none of it.

"I wouldn't."

"PLEASE TELL me you strutted your sexy looking self down the hallway, and he stared at you the entire time."

Rae chuckled at Liv's comment as she scrolled through one of the online dating apps she had on her phone. Seeing nothing of interest, she placed the phone down and noticed that all eyes were on her. She nodded and grinned.

"That's my girl!" exclaimed Eve, which might have been the loudest she had ever heard Eve speak. The girls held up their drinks to cheers, brought their glasses to their lips, then placed them back down on the table in front of them. Liv had called an emergency happy hour session at the Green Hat after she heard the news about Flint. Rae didn't see the text until she was about to leave the office, but changed her plans and headed to the Green Hat to hang out with her girls. After all, she was probably just going to sit on her couch and watch some episodes of a show she had already seen a million times.

"So, Danielle has no idea that you guys dated?" Eve took another sip of her drink before dabbing a napkin on her lips.

Rae shook her head. "Nope. And based on her reaction when she entered my office after Flint, he didn't tell her either. Plus, I don't know how that would come up in conversation at work."

"Touché."

"So, now what?" Jules asked. She glanced around the bar, but her eyes landed back on Rae.

"I assume he will contact me. If I had to guess, he won't keep this professional either."

"Not based on what you said," snickered Liv. Rae glared at her, which made Liv giggle harder. "I'm just sayin'." She placed a chip laced with spinach and artichoke dip into her mouth.

"I'm not mentally prepared for how awkward this is going to be."

"It will be okay. Both of you are adults and will push aside any differences to solve any issues that come up while you work together." Rae could always count on Jules to be optimistic about a situation.

"Yeah, something or *someone* will have some things resolved, but I'm not sure that it will be WPWL's administrative policies." If glares could kill, Liv would be face-first into the dip she was snacking on.

Eve shook her head at Liv. "Anyway, I'm curious to see how this will go. Did Danielle send that email connecting the two of you yet?"

Rae nodded. "She sent it a few minutes after I left work to come here."

"And nothing from Flint yet?"

Rae shook her head. "Not yet. And even if he had sent something, I would wait to read it at work tomorrow."

Liv stood up and clapped for Rae. Rae shook her head and said, "One day, you'll be in a similar situation, and I will laugh at you. With a capital *L*."

"Yeah, yeah. When hell freezes over, and you get a guest spot on *Sesame Street*." Liv waved her off.

The rest of the table giggled at Liv's antics before the topic changed.

"How's the packing going?" Jules asked.

"To be honest, not well. I was planning on working on it this weekend. This week has been mentally exhausting because of work." Rae's three friends nodded in sympathy.

Before anyone could say anything else, John appeared at their table with four drinks and told them it was on the house. When they protested, he shook his head and smiled. After the women thanked him, they each took sips of their new drink as he walked away.

"This is so refreshing. We need to tell John that this needs to be on the menu as soon as possible," Eve said as the rest of the group nodded.

"Yeah, he can name it after me."

"Of course he can, Liv. Of course he can." Eve shook her head as she continued to enjoy her drink.

"Anyway, this might be off base, but maybe Flint would offer to help you move."

Rae turned her body in Jules's direction and tilted her head. "How would he know I'm moving, Jules?"

"I might have mentioned it to Flint."

Rae closed her eyes before opening them once more. "I thought you said you didn't talk to him that long."

"I didn't, but you know, sometimes when I get startled or nervous, I blurt things out and then I don't realize what I'm saying until it's already too late. Like I'm doing right now." Jules took a deep breath after the rush of words came flying out of her mouth.

Rae reached over and patted her hand. "It's fine." And it

was. He hadn't reached out to contact her, so she wasn't going to worry about it.

"It just came up when we talked about some people we knew back when we were kids. It was after I told him what you were up to—"

"Jules, seriously, don't worry about it. It's fine." Rae offered a small smile. "The ball is in his court."

5
____

The next day, Rae woke up to the sound of her alarm. Trying to shake the grogginess and minor hangover she had from their happy hour, Rae sat up in bed and stretched. She checked her phone and saw a text notification. Her heart skipped a beat but quickly settled down when she saw the text was from Eve.

Eve: Anything from Flint?

Eve freaked her out because of how well she knew her after all of these years.

Rae: No, why?

Eve: Because I know you've probably been racking your brain all night trying to figure out what to do if he contacted you.

"Touché," whispered Rae as she wandered into the bathroom.

Rae: It wasn't all night...only part of the night, thank you very much.

Eve: Semantics. How are you taking it?

Realizing she would be late for work if she didn't get a move on, Rae put a shower cap on her head and jumped into the shower. She was out in fifteen minutes and finished up the rest of her morning routine in record time. Rae chose a dark green dress and brown knee-high boots to wear to work that morning. She grabbed her brown pea coat before haphazardly placing her hair into a ponytail. Double-checking to make sure she had everything she needed, she locked her front door and headed to the metro station.

As she walked to the metro, she couldn't help but smile as the thought this being one of the last weeks she would have to make this long trek to work. Rae lived in DuPont Circle and had to take two trains to make it to her office in Arlington. Her commute was about forty to fifty minutes if the trains were running on time each way, and she was tired of it. The only thing keeping her going was that her move was happening soon, meaning that her hellish commute would all be over soon.

About sixty minutes later, Rae was sitting down at her desk and reviewing her schedule for the day and the rest of the week. She had to put her final touches on the policy slides for Danielle to check for the board meeting and had a few meetings with her boss and the CEO of their company. Rae took a moment to close her eyes and take a few deep breaths, and then she opened her eyes and headed to the kitchen to get a cup of coffee to start her day right. As she waited for her coffee to finish brewing, she realized she hadn't responded to Eve's text message.

Rae: *I'm okay, I guess. Seeing him in person yesterday was shocking, to say the least.*

Eve didn't respond right away, so Rae grabbed her coffee from the break room and headed back to her desk, waving at a couple of people she passed on the way. She sat down in front of her laptop and was ready to get to work.

Her work and meetings kept her busy until she could break for a late lunch. She grabbed her coat and walked outside to one of the food trucks that hadn't yet packed up their equipment. She ordered a sandwich and checked her phone as she waited for her food.

Eve: Yeah, I can see how that could be a shock. I'm not surprised that he attempted to hunt you down after his meeting at your office.

Rae: Why is that?

While Rae waited for Eve to answer back, she checked the group chat that all the girls were on, but it was eerily quiet when it was usually bursting with activity. She quickly typed out a message in that chat before turning her attention back to her conversation with Eve.

Eve: Given how things ended with you guys, I'm shocked he approached Jules about it. Asking about her family and making small talk with her about the people they grew up with is one thing; talking about you is another. But the article and now his behavior makes me think he is trying to make amends and potentially get into your life again. Of course, this is if the article is about your relationship with him.

Rae: That makes sense. But I guess we'll never know unless he contacts me. I'm sure it will happen at some point soon.

Eve: That's true. Do you want him to contact you? On a personal level.

Rae: Yes, and no. Part of me wants to talk to him to get a better sense of closure, but I think leaving things in the past might be for the best.

*Eve: Those are excellent points. Although I hate speaking for *other people, I know I can speak for the other girls, so I want to reiterate that we have your back. No matter what you do.*

With that, Rae smiled, collected her lunch, and headed back to her desk to get more work done.

LATER THAT EVENING, Rae breathed a sigh of relief when she sat down on her couch at 8:00 p.m. She had just gotten home from work, and all she wanted to do was to go to bed again.

"I don't know if I have ever been as happy to see Friday in my entire life," she mumbled as she got up and hung up her coat in the hall closet. She then went to her room and changed into her pj's before heading back out to the kitchen. She grabbed a pint of ice cream from the freezer and turned on one of her favorite reality TV shows and vegged out. During a commercial break, she picked up her phone and checked her messages. Seeing nothing of importance, she opened up the application with her contacts and scrolled until she found Flint West's phone number. Although she knew the best course of action was to place her phone down, something was urging her to call him.

Shaking her head, she tossed her phone onto the couch and continued eating her ice cream. About an hour later, she wandered into her bathroom and standing at the counter, stared at herself in the mirror. She could see some hint of the sleepless night she'd had last night. She played with the bags under her eyes that were kind of noticeable against her golden-brown skin. She glanced down at her phone and sighed at herself. Rae's obsession with her phone began the moment she heard Danielle had connected them via email.

"Get over yourself, Rae," she said to herself as she started her bedtime routine. As she was getting into bed, she tried to resist the urge to check her phone once more.

"Put the phone down and go to bed," she muttered. Of course, she didn't listen to herself because the next thing she knew, she was checking up on the group chat in which she, Liv, Jules, and Eve talked. As she was about to close the app, her phone buzzed.

It wasn't a text message, but an email. Rae's heart rolled around in her throat when she saw that the message was from Flint West.

To: Rachelle Carter
From: Flint West
Subject: Meeting

Are you available to meet at your office on Monday to talk about the objectives Danielle laid out in her email? Just about any time works for me.

Thanks,

Flint

Rae's eyes darted to the clock on her phone and she saw that it was almost ten. Why was he emailing her this late? And on a Friday night? She knew for a fact that the project they were working on together didn't require them to meet right away. Rae hoped to meet after she'd moved and finished up with the board meeting.

She sent a short email asking why he wanted to meet on

Monday, and that it would require some heavy lifting on her end. Then she mentioned that she'd get back to him with a time, but thought later next week or the following week would work better with her schedule. There. That would buy her some time before she had to face him.

As she was about to turn her phone on do not disturb, another buzz stopped her in her tracks. She flipped back to her inbox and saw that Flint had sent her another email.

According to him, it was dire because things needed to start moving ahead of WPWL's board meeting. But meeting Monday wasn't going to work for Rae because she needed to make preparations for their meeting. Professionally and personally. She told him that in another email before quickly putting her phone on do not disturb and went to bed.

Rae woke up the next morning feeling refreshed. Most mornings that came only after several cups of coffee, so she would take it. She grabbed her phone and headed into the kitchen. Once she started her coffeemaker, she turned her attention to the clock over her oven. There was plenty of time for her to head to a barre class if there were any spots available.

She checked her phone and signed up for a class that would start in two hours, giving her plenty of time to get herself together. When she closed the barre studio's app, she noticed she had a text message. Thinking one of the girls might have sent a text at some point, she opened her messages. Her eyes widened as she read the text.

Flint: Figured it might be easier to text. What's wrong with a meeting on Monday?

So this was how he was going to play it.

Rae: As I mentioned in the email, I'd need to make preparations for the meeting. What documents do you need so I can get them together? I won't be ready to meet on this short notice.

There. End of that.

She quickly sent a message to her girlfriends, stating that Flint had reached out to her before she hopped into the shower.

Once she changed into her workout gear, she reached over and checked her phone.

Flint: Danielle wanted us to meet on Monday after I meet with her.

Rae threw back her head and held in a scream. Monday it was.

6

———

Rae tapped her pen on the table in one of the conference rooms at work on Monday afternoon. The plan was to have Flint meet her in this room after he wrapped up his meeting with Danielle. She couldn't wait to get this meeting finished. Although she was curious about what he'd been up to over the years, she'd realized that just being within four feet of him was enough to short-circuit her brain and lead her to probably saying something she should have kept to herself.

It was 12:57 p.m., according to Rae's laptop. She had spent most of the morning, pulling together potential files for their meeting. Still, she felt as if she was looking for a needle in a haystack. A few more taps of the pen drove her to the brink of insanity so she put it down and looked through her phone to find something to entertain her while she waited.

"You look busy."

Rae jumped at the sound of his voice but played it off. She glanced at the time and saw that it was 12:59 p.m. Of course, he wouldn't be late. He never was.

"I was, and you interrupted me, which in many cultures is rude... Hi, Flint."

"Rae. It's nice to see you again."

"You saw me on Thursday."

"You know what I mean. How have you been doing? Changing the world for the better?"

Rae knew he wasn't being sarcastic with that compliment, but let his words roll off her like water off a duck's back. She shook her head at the image.

"Thanks. I heard you weren't doing too bad yourself. Pick a seat, and we can get started. Do you want any water? I can grab some for you. It won't take long."

"I'm good, and thanks. I think I'll sit right here." Rae watched as he walked around the table and picked a seat to the right of her.

"I'm going to be blunt. Why pick that seat out of all the seats in this room?"

"Well, I don't have my laptop with me, and I figured it would be easier to look over your shoulder versus you having to turn your laptop around to face me whenever you wanted to show me something." The smirk Flint sent her way sent shivers down her spine. That smirk led to quite a few long nights when they... She cleared her brain for the second time to prevent herself from going down that route again.

"Trust me, turning my laptop around for you wouldn't be a hardship."

He didn't reply for a moment, and she didn't know how close he was to her until she felt his breath on the back of her neck.

"But where's the fun in that?"

She could confirm that he still wore the same cologne

that he wore five years ago. Rae closed her eyes as the scent brought back wonderful memories from their time together and how she missed him after his scent remained on her sheets. Blinking her eyes a few times to remove those thoughts from the front of her brain, Rae turned back to her computer and started typing an email. She didn't have to send it right that second, but it gave her something to do while she thought of what to say. But before Rae could say anything, Flint moved back and placed the notepad he had brought with him on the table. She could hear him rifling through his notes; it was taking him a long time to find whatever he was looking for to share with her.

"So, how have you been?"

"Not too bad. Working a lot. I got my master's degree two years ago. Overall, I would say I'm doing pretty well. How about yourself?"

"Well, I'm a lawyer and started working for the same firm as my dad. I moved back here, and I've been working and volunteering when I can to keep me busy when work doesn't."

"That sounds like a great plan. I need to volunteer more, but I still do barre classes in my spare time."

"Still? I'm glad you kept up with it because it was something you loved when—" Flint cut himself off. He cleared his throat. "Anyway, I'm here to talk about some of the work I'm doing with WPWL."

"Yes. So what's up, and why couldn't it wait?"

"Most of the things related to this I'm working with Danielle on."

Flint now had her full and undivided attention. "Then why are we meeting? Are you trying to waste my time?"

"No. The short answer is that there might be quite a bit of restructuring going on within Wild Parks, Wild Lands, and their Board of Directors, and we might need documents and other items on short notice. There haven't been any lawsuits yet, but we are trying to prevent one. Danielle thought you would be the best person for the job."

Rae's hands flew up to her face. She stopped just short of rubbing her hands over her eyes in frustration because she didn't want to look like a raccoon if she smudged her makeup. "So, this is pretty serious."

"Yep and the information will be based on all of the things that I'm allowed to tell you. The project might become tedious, but we can do it. Together."

"What have I gotten myself into?" Rae asked as she looked around her apartment. It was the weekend after she met with Flint. She was sitting on the floor in the middle of her living room, tabulating what she needed to do to prepare for her upcoming move.

"Why did I decide to move this month?" Although nothing but silence answered her question, it confirmed what she already knew.

She looked around her and decided which things she needed for the next couple of weeks and which things she could start packing away. Rae finished wrapping the first few items and placing them a cardboard box labeled "Living Room" when her phone rang. Liv's name popped up on her phone's screen.

"Hello?"

"Open the door." What in the world was going on?

Rae looked through her door's peephole before opening the door, standing there dumbfounded as Eve and Liv greeted her with big smiles.

"What are you two doing here? Where's Jules?"

"We knew you needed help with packing, so we figured we would come over now and maybe do a barre class afterward? Hence the workout clothes we're wearing. Jules had a family event to attend, but I think she might have just said that to get out of helping us. Kidding!" Rae knew that Eve was kidding since Jules was usually the first one to volunteer to help anyone.

"You guys are too sweet. Let me grab more packing tape and markers, and we can get to packing. Everything else is already in the living room."

"We know," Liv called after her.

Rae grabbed the extra supplies, and the three women got to work. After a few hours, the friends decided that there was no way they were making it to the barre class that day. Instead, they ordered pizza and grabbed a bottle of wine from Rae's kitchen to open when the pizza arrived. Just as Eve opened the bottle of wine, the pizza arrived. Liv brought the pizza to Rae's dining room table as Eve was pouring wine for each person.

"So I meant to say something earlier, but I went on this date with this guy and—" Rae's phone cut off Liv's comment. Liv continued with her story, but Rae wasn't paying attention since the text she'd received distracted her.

"Rae, what's up?"

"Um. Read this." Rae placed her phone on the table and Eve and Liv leaned over to look at it.

"I was going to ask you if he reached out to you. I must be psychic."

Eve playfully rolled her eyes at Liv. "Let me know when you can predict Lotto numbers." She turned to Rae and said, "I guess I thought he would have texted you right after he talked to Jules, so I figured he just decided not to say anything."

"I forgot to mention that he emailed and texted me before this. When planning something for work," said Rae. Eve softly shoved her shoulder. "What?"

"Why didn't you tell us?"

"I forgot. My bad." She turned her attention back to the text.

Flint: I wanted to ask if you wanted to get together for drinks sometime? For old times' sake? This is unrelated to work.

"I'm not sure what I should say."

"Surprisingly, neither do I. I mean the answer is usually yes, no, or maybe, but which answer should you pick? Who knows, and either answer might make it awkward when you have to see him at work. However, I do know more wine is in order." Eve stood up and walked into Rae's small kitchen to retrieve a second bottle from Rae's wine rack. She opened it with ease and refilled their glasses.

The three sat in silence after Eve sat down in her seat. The longer everyone was quiet, the more time she had to process the text message.

"You know this isn't even that big of a deal. It's just a drink."

"Yeah, with an ex that you haven't heard from in years. That broke your heart by ignoring you instead of being a decent human being and telling you in person, especially after you had been together for over a year." Liv snapped. Rae was taken aback and shifted her gaze from Liv to Eve, where she saw her other friend nodding her head along.

"That's a hard pill to swallow."

"Rae, I didn't mean it like that—"

"No, it's fine. You're right. I should keep things professional. After all, what we had was over a long time ago. In hindsight, I'm surprised we lasted as long as we did. We were just a mess."

"You guys were young, had fallen in love, and then he moved away. The fact that you made it for over a year long distance was amazing." Eve gently laid a hand on Rae's shoulder.

Rae nodded and rubbed her hands together. These interactions with him plus talking about it with the girls were bringing back so many memories. Not that she hadn't thought about him since they broke up, but hearing from him brought up thoughts and feelings she didn't know she still had.

"Do you know what you're going to do?" Eve asked as she leaned forward in her seat.

Rae shook her head. "I don't think meeting with him alone outside of a professional capacity is in the cards right now. But I'm also polite enough not to leave him on read so I'll come up with a response to his message."

"Fair." Liv swirled her wine around in her glass.

"What do you think, Eve?"

"I don't blame you for not wanting to see him. Even if it's been years. I wouldn't want to see my exes either. Especially given how you guys ended." Liv nodded her head in agreement as Eve continued. "To play devil's advocate, maybe going out with him to catch up wouldn't be the worst thing in the world? Sometimes you have to leave things in the past, but other times you can leaving the door open to a second chance. I'm not saying date him again if that's what he wants, but at the very least you can show him how well you're doing and get the closure you need."

Rae shrugged but didn't have a response, as she stood up and walked to her living room window. She gazed out to the street below and took several deep breaths. Being back in the same city as Flint would be interesting. She knew that at some point, she would see him again, whether on purpose or by chance. However, she wanted to buy herself enough time to decide, and right now, too many things were going on, including him entering her life. Rae pulled out her phone and composed a message to Flint.

Rae: *I'm super busy with work and moving at the moment, but maybe we can get together for drinks sometime in the future.*

She reread what she typed before reading it out loud to Liv and Eve.

"That sounds good."

"Yeah. It isn't closing the door, but it's pushing a personal reunion down the road. And since you aren't against meeting up for drinks, I think that's the right thing to do. Also, it won't make things awkward when you have to see or talk to one another for work."

Rae agreed and pressed send. She then put her phone on silent and facedown on the dining room table. "I know I'll be obsessing over it as is. I don't need to stare at my phone screen besides that."

"Makes sense. Do you want to pack more?" Liv stood up and stretched. Rae and Eve joined her, and the three packed for a few more hours before Eve and Liv had to leave. The ladies promised they would come back to help and would drag Jules along with them as Rae walked them to the door. After Rae shut the door behind them, she brought their wine glasses in the kitchen to be washed, but couldn't remove her gaze from her phone. Should she check to see if Flint texted her back? She took several more steps before turning around again to stare at her phone. Rae repeated the motion before rolling her eyes at herself.

She set the wine glasses next to the sink and walked back over to her phone. There was a text notification from Flint. Taking a deep breath, Rae read the message.

Flint: Oh that's right. Jules mentioned that when I saw her last.

Well, she knew she didn't have to reply to that so she placed her phone back on the table and went about cleaning up the mess they had made.

She checked the time. Noticing that it was getting late, she headed to her living room to watch some television before bed.

Flint: If you need any help moving, let me know. I'm happy to help. Looking forward to that drink at some point.

Rae left him on read and continued to relax for the rest of the night.

"Guess what?" The voice paused as he looked up from his screen and watched Rae settle into her couch.

The voice on the other end of the phone didn't respond right away.

"What happened?"

"Flint is talking to Rae Carter again."

The gasp and loud boom on the phone made him think she might have fainted. That had not been his intent, but he knew that she needed to know the truth. He patiently waited for her to get herself together. "Are you okay?"

"I'm fine. I thought we were in the clear once Flint moved back to the area."

"Should I go back to plan A? And then go from there?"

"Sounds like a plan. Let me know how it goes."

"Will do."

7

"So, I saw Flint again." All heads in the room swerved to Jules as she broke the silence in the room. The ladies were busy helping Rae bring a few things into her new apartment and unpack what they could fit into her and Jules's cars.

Rae said, "Oh, really? How is he?" She hoped the sweat that was now forming on her golden-brown skin wouldn't raise any suspicions since she'd been moving boxes around. She wiped her arm across her forehead and kept walking.

It had been about a week since she last heard from him in person or over text. They had shared a couple of emails back and forth about work-related things and that had annoyed her more than she would like to admit.

"He's doing good. He mentioned he reached out to you about getting drinks with him."

"Yep." Rae offered no explanation other than that. She slammed the box she was carrying down on the kitchen counter a little harder than necessary. She busied herself by removing the tape and placing some smaller utensils and tools into where she wanted them in the kitchen.

"Well, since she won't ask, what did he say?" Liv asked from her place on the floor. She was resting after doing her share of clearing out the two vehicles.

"I think he was trying to figure out what we were up to over the last few years. He focused on Rae, of course, but he seemed genuine. We chatted for a while at this event this time around because we lost our parents in the crowd."

"What event was this?" Rae thanked Liv in her head for asking one of the questions she was thinking of asking.

"This was a political fundraiser. Virginia state politics."

"Was he there for his firm or with his father?" Rae figured she could take over the questioning at this point.

"I think he was Terry's plus-one. I didn't see Gladys at all, and she loves attending these events."

Rae's eyebrow rose at Jules's explanation. Mentioning his parents didn't bring warm, fuzzy feelings to Rae. She held nothing against them, but there was a level of indifference from his mother that didn't rest easy with her. His dad was nice, so she couldn't complain. It was interesting that Flint was attending political fundraisers, according to the article. It wasn't work-related if he was attending as his father's plus-one.

"Have you thought more about going out to drinks with him?"

"No." *That was a lie.*

"You sure about that?" Liv jumped into the conversation like a barrel of dynamite.

"Yep." *Still a lie.*

"Well, think about it now." The glare that Rae was giving

Liv could set snow on fire in the North Pole. "Do you have an answer now? Just admit that you want to see him again." Liv met Rae's glare with a stare of her own.

"Fine. I wouldn't mind getting a drink with Flint. For closure's sake. But maybe it should happen after we finish this project together at work." Rae saw Eve's eyes light up. Jules let out a deep breath, while Liv's mouth was agape.

"I knew it. Now text Flint and tell him so. You don't have any other excuses."

"Oh. I didn't realize that moving wasn't a good excuse."

"It's a good excuse now. Won't be an excuse in a couple of weeks. Doesn't mean that you can't text him now to set something up."

Rae couldn't argue with that logic. She pulled her phone from her back pocket and scrolled down to the text message thread with Flint. Her fingers hovered over her screen as she thought about what to say. Taking a deep breath, she typed the message that Eve had been waiting for her to send.

Rae: When are you available to grab drinks?

Rae put her phone down on the kitchen counter and stuck her tongue out at Liv.

"Mature."

Before Rae could respond, her phone pinged.

"Well, that was quick," Rae mumbled as she picked up her phone.

Flint: Would tomorrow work for you?

"He wants to go out tomorrow."

"Wow. Talk about moving fast." Eve said as she stood up and moved toward another box in the corner. Jules made her way over to help Eve put her things away with Rae's direction.

"I can't do tomorrow, but maybe next Saturday."

Rae: I'm moving into my new apartment tomorrow. How about next Saturday unless something comes up?

She still needed that escape plan just in case.

Flint: That works. Do you need any help moving tomorrow? I'm free.

Rae: I think we can manage. I hired movers.

Flint: It wouldn't be an issue at all. I'm happy to help.

Rae couldn't find the words to get her feelings across to her friends. "He offered to help me move tomorrow. And kept the offer on the table even after I told him I'd hired movers."

"Another set of hands wouldn't hurt." Eve smirked and shared a glance with Jules and Liv.

"What do you three know that I don't?"

"What? I have no idea what you're talking about."

Jules shrugged as Liv shook her head.

"You're full of it, but I'll find out what y'all are hiding. One way or another."

Liv began singing that very song, which further drove Rae to the brink of insanity. She closed her eyes and rubbed her temples. When Liv stopped laughing, Rae chimed in, "Good attempt at changing the subject, but not slick enough. I guess I shouldn't turn down extra help. But I want to know what you guys know that I don't."

"Let's just say; we might have made sure he was free tomorrow no matter what. He was keen to help."

Rae knew that her eyes would get stuck on the ceiling if she rolled them one more time was, in fact, true and not an empty threat that her mom used to say when she caught her rolling her eyes.

Rae: Sure. Here's the address to my soon-to-be old apartment. We're starting at 9:00 a.m. sharp.

Flint: *I'll be there at 8:55 a.m.*

THE KNOCK on the door stopped Rae midstep. It was moving day and she was already over everything. She turned around and headed back toward her front door. Looking through the peephole, she took a step back.

"Right on time," she mumbled as she checked the time on her phone. Taking a deep breath, she swung open the door.

"Hey," was the first thing that fell from her lips.

"Hey, back at you."

She moved out of the way to let him into the apartment. He was wearing a black T-shirt and sweatpants, attire that she was sure would be comfortable enough to help her move in. As he walked by her, she got a whiff of his cologne. She thought it was weird to wear it when it was almost a guarantee that you'd be sweating, but whatever, it was his body.

Rae didn't try to be discreet as she scanned his body from head to toe. The way the shirt hugged his chest was a sin that she was willing to commit. The sweatpants were hiding his lower half, which was an immoral act too. They must have been having the same thoughts because she noticed that his eyes were sweeping across her body. Interesting.

"Welcome to my humble abode. Can I get you something to drink? I'm planning on having beer and pizza for everyone at my new apartment."

"I'm good, thanks."

"Thanks for coming over to help me move."

"Happy to help. Anything new going on?"

"Nope. Most of my life has revolved around organizing

this move. Thanks for sending over that information I needed for the documents I needed to hunt down for you."

Flint paused and placed his hands in his pockets. "Don't mention it."

Rae could feel the awkwardness as she walked to a stack of boxes and grabbed the spreadsheet from on top of them. She reviewed the information about which boxes went where at her new apartment. Looking at this spreadsheet served as a way to prevent Rae from having to make conversation with Flint and stop her from saying something she might regret.

She could cut the tension in the room with a knife. Before Rae or Flint could say anything, there was a knock on the door.

"Perfect timing," Rae muttered. She took a deep breath as she opened the door. In walked Eve and Liv, the latter attempting to stretch her limbs as if getting ready to run a race. She stopped her movements once she noticed that Rae was not alone in her apartment.

"Long time, no see, Flint," Liv said, breaking the silence. Rae sensed the tension defusing and she felt a small weight lift off of her shoulders. She would get through this day. "By the way, Jules will be over in twenty to thirty minutes. She had to take care of something at home last minute."

"Yeah, it has been a bit, hasn't it?" Flint said. He gave Liv a small smile and turned his attention to the apartment. Liv walked over to him and started a discussion as they walked around the apartment, analyzing how much stuff Rae had to move.

"Thank goodness for Liv," Rae said as she strolled over to Eve.

"That's an understatement. I got lucky and found a

parking spot behind your car, but can move for the moving truck."

"Oh, they can just park near the divide over there. You know, Flint didn't need to come."

"Well, that was a swift change of subject. We both know what was on your mind."

"I—uh—I," Rae stuttered as she tried to come up with something to say that would make a good defense. Nothing came. "Yep, that's on my mind. Especially because now I feel like he's pushing himself into my life, and I'm not exactly denying him. And could you whisper? They're only in the next room."

Rae's phone buzzed, and she saw a text from Jules.

Jules: Sorry, I am running late! I should be there soon. And I need to talk to you about Flint.

"I'm glad you admitted it. Anyway, I completely agree. There is no reason for Flint being here besides the fact that he wanted to be here."

"Do you know why Jules would want to talk to me about Flint again?" Rae hoped her friends had talked to each other before they came over because she was dying to find out what was going on.

"I hoped that Jules would be here to tell you because she's the one who has all the information. I wanted you to hear it straight from the horse's mouth, or however, the saying goes. And this is not me calling Jules a horse, that was just me using a common phrase, but I might have gotten it wrong—"

"Just tell me what's up, please." Rae kept the bite out of her voice, even though she was getting frustrated with Eve's stalling. Her phone buzzed again and she assumed it was Jules. She looked down and read the notification.

Unknown Number: *You will regret talking to Flint again.*

"So Flint has been contacting Jules and talking about you a lot. Wait that came out wrong. I don't mean that he's been doing it to be a creep. I mean, he's been trying to catch up on what he missed, I guess?"

Rae didn't respond because she was stuck on the message she had just received. What was she going to do with this? Telling Eve might be the best bet, but what would happen? She could block the number, but the person would just find a new number and send her messages. Second-guessing herself too many times was about to lead her down a giant rabbit hole and she needed that to end.

"Rae, are you listening to me?"

"Sorry, I got distracted by my phone. What did you say?"

Eve's patience was wearing thin, but she repeated what she'd said. "Well, it's more than just that. He's been getting advice from her too."

"Advice about what he should do about me?"

Eve nodded but said nothing.

"Huh. Looks like Jules and I need to chat."

"Are you mad at her?"

Rae thought for a second before shaking her head. "No, I'm not mad. Confused about why she didn't tell me this was happening, but not angry about it. She's also been very distracted lately and forgetting to mention things unless something else triggers a memory about it. I'm curious about that too, and I hope nothing is wrong with her."

"Understandable."

And with that, there was a knock on the door.

"Bets on whether it's the movers or Jules?" Rae asked as she put her hand on the doorknob.

"Jules!" Eve said as Rae swung open the door. In walked Jules with a smile on her face.

"Sorry I'm late, but I didn't run into much traffic and the lights were on my side, so I'm here a little earlier than I thought I would be!"

"I'm a better psychic than Liv. I'll figure out my own lotto numbers." Eve smirked at Rae.

"Uh-huh, keep telling yourself that." She ignored the glare from Eve and smiled at Jules and whispered, "We have a little time, but do you want to tell me about what's going on with Flint? This might be the only moment we have today between the craziness that's about to ensue."

"Sure. So, Flint has been talking to me about you ever since you decided that he could come and help with the move. I thought that was interesting since he didn't text me after we saw each other at a couple of events over the last few weeks. Anyway, based on what he said, I think he thinks the door to getting to know you again has been opened a bit with you allowing him to help you move. Now he hasn't explicitly said anything that confirms this, but his texts show otherwise." As she was saying these words, Jules pulled out her phone and showed Rae the messages between her and Flint.

Rae read through the texts and got the same impression that Jules had. He seemed excited that she wanted his help. This was a change from how she imagined he would have acted several years ago when he thrived on being cool, calm, and collected at all costs.

"Thanks for sharing—" Rae's words were cut off by Liv and Flint entering the room.

"I can't wait to see what Rae does with her new place. I'm

sure it will look great. Oh, hey, Jules! Didn't know you were here."

"Just walked through the door about a minute ago," Jules said as Rae handed her back her phone. "Rae, have you heard anything from the movers?"

Rae shook her head as she pulled out her phone to double-check if she had received a message from them. "Let's see. They are about ten minutes late, so maybe I'll give them another five before calling the company." She had been keeping track of the time but got distracted when the conversation had switched to Flint.

"Sounds good."

"Before I forget, thank y'all for coming and helping today. It means so much to me." The group told Rae not to worry about it and she smiled at each woman before her eyes landed on Flint. When his eyes connected with hers, she felt an electric current run through her veins. She saw the past and present in his eyes. But was there a potential future there? The sound of her phone ringing forced her to break their eye contact.

"Hello?" Rae breathed a sigh of relief when she realized it was the movers she had hired to help her get to from DC to Arlington. But that relief was short-lived.

"What do you mean you're overbooked? You've got to be kidding me!" The anger was billowing off of her in droves. "Thanks for your time," Rae said as she hung up the phone. She took several deep breaths before she could form the words to explain in more detail what she had just learned.

"Well, it looks like I won't be moving today. The movers overbooked themselves by mistake."

"Overbooked?" Liv asked, not believing what Rae had said. All Rae did was nod. She took out her ponytail and let her wavy hair roam free. She was getting a headache, and removing her ponytail provided some temporary relief.

"We'll figure something out," Jules said, forever the optimist. But Rae didn't hear her. The deep breaths that she took earlier were for naught. Her anger was building once again, no matter how much she wanted to stay calm. She knew she would have to find a new moving company if there were any available and pay more in fees to get her stuff moved in today or tomorrow. Thankfully, her lease wasn't up today, so if they needed to push it to sometime during the week, she could manage if she could book a bigger truck. She would just have to take off another day or two from work, which would be another pain. As she was about to research movers, Flint stepped forward.

"Wait. I might have an idea."

Rae looked up from her phone and she was sure he could see the tears in her eyes. "What are you thinking?"

"I need to make a few phone calls, but I might be able to get a few people to come down and help. We have what, four cars available? You would probably only need to book a U-Haul truck for the bigger furniture, but we could probably manage most of the stuff on our own. You would just need to hope that we can find a U-Haul big enough."

Rae's gaze never left his as she realized what he was suggesting. Although it would be harder to move, and there were a lot of what-if factors involved, if everything worked out, she could still move today. She figured she owed Flint her life's savings if they could pull this off. Not that there was a lot in her savings, anyway.

Jules spoke up before Rae could. "That could work." Jules turned to Rae and placed a hand on her shoulder. "I know how disappointing it can be not to be able to do something that you wanted to do."

Eve leaned over and whispered in Rae's ear, "I can see the internal debate you're having with yourself about taking Flint's help. Just go with the flow and try not to overanalyze it."

Rae pondered her options before she turned to Flint and said, "Okay. Please call in the reinforcements." Flint beamed and walked outside to make a few phone calls.

"I think you just made his entire year. It was kind of hot watching him take charge like that," Liv said as she turned to look at her friends.

"I don't know about all of that, but it's making me think more about grabbing drinks with him. Which is a shitty thing to think."

"What do you mean?" Jules asked.

"So I'm still on the fence about this whole going-out-for-drinks thing even though it's us just going to grab drinks...for old times' sake."

"Or it could mean something?" Liv smirked at Rae and earned a glare in return.

"Anyway, now I'm thinking about going to the bar with him because he's offering to go more out of his way to help me move today. And that's not how I want to view it."

"I know it's hard not to view it that way, but you shouldn't, and he probably doesn't think that you should go out with him because he is doing this for you either. He doesn't seem to be trying to force you to do anything that you don't want to do."

"I guess I'll have to talk to him about it. But for now, we should relax a bit until we see if Flint can get reinforcements to help."

The friends chatted while they waited for Flint to return. The minutes felt like hours for Rae as she hoped he would have good news when he walked back through the door. To take her mind off of her impatience, she looked around her apartment and thought about all the memories she shared here over the last couple of years.

"Hey. Do y'all remember when we all got drunk and tried to make a chocolate cake?"

Jules's eyes widened while Liv burst out laughing.

"I try to forget about that night. The amount of alcohol that we drank was...whew." Eve shook her head at the memory.

"Didn't we screw the recipe up by adding too much sugar?"

Eve nodded, and Jules responded, "Yep. I think I was hungover for a week straight."

"Yeah. That was a lot of fun, but I can't party like that anymore. But you know what I loved most about it? We were hanging out together in our yoga pants."

"She won't admit it, but she was happier about being in her yoga pants." Liv smirked at Rae, who gave her the one-finger salute.

Before Rae and Liv could get into it, Flint opened the door and walked into the apartment. His eyes found Rae and he told her, "We are in business. I have a few friends coming to help. Two of them will head over and grab the U-Haul truck, so you don't have to worry about that. We booked everything, and we're ready to go."

Rae squealed and darted over to Flint. She hopped into his arms and gave him a huge hug before she could process what she was doing. When she realized what she had done, she had somehow ended up with her legs wrapped around Flint's waist, and he was helping to hold her up by gripping her lower back. A few seconds later, she let her legs drop and took a small step away from him. His hands were still on her lower back, which she assumed had been instinctual.

"I—I'm sorry about that. Thanks for doing that." She stepped away from him, but Flint didn't release his grip.

"Don't worry about it. I'm glad we could make this happen."

"I can send you the money for the U-Haul truck."

"Don't worry about it."

Rae leaned forward an inch. "What do you mean, don't worry about it?"

"Don't worry about it."

"Flint, this—"

"I'm trying to take one thing off your plate. If you want to argue about it later, that's fine, but we should spend more time figuring out how we'll pull this move off."

Rae nodded and Flint removed his hands from her back. She missed the sensation of his hands holding her up. "So when are your friends getting here?" She hoped the conversation would stick to being about her move instead of focusing on what she'd just done.

"I'm not sure how long it would take the group to get the U-Haul truck, but the other four guys should be over in about thirty minutes. We can load the cars we have, and more than likely by the time they are packed up, the group of four should be here. We can load up the two cars they're bringing too."

Rae was having a hard time keeping up with what was going on because everything seemed to be happening so fast. For that, she was happy he was taking charge, but she felt some way about him stepping in and running the show. This was her move, and Rae had organized things. But the things she'd put together had fallen through, so she should just be happy that she could still move today. The internal debate she was having in her head raged on and the thoughts didn't stop until Eve spoke up.

"How were you able to get your friends to come on short notice?"

Flint turned to her and smiled before saying, "They owe me a favor. Plus, I mentioned that there might be pizza and alcohol when we finish. You'd be surprised how free food and alcohol can entice people even in their late twenties or thirties." Flint turned to Rae and said, "Don't worry, I can pay for the extra food and alcohol."

Rae didn't reply. She nodded and made a mental note to pull Flint aside and talk to him about all of this. "If everyone is okay, let's pack up these cars."

The women and Flint got to work moving boxes from the apartment down to the cars. As Flint had predicted, by the time they finished, two-thirds of the reinforcements that Flint had called had arrived with two more cars. Rae profusely thanked the guys, and they began loading up the cars. When they finished, the U-Haul truck had arrived. And out popped a familiar face.

"Kane?!" Rae shouted as she ran up to him and hugged him. She knew that Flint and he had been best friends when they were dating, but didn't realize they had stayed in touch after Flint's stationing in Denver. They had hung out a few times while she and Flint were together, but she hadn't seen him since. She turned back to look at Eve, whom she knew had had a small thing with Kane a few years ago, to see her reaction. Eve stared at Kane with her mouth agape. It was one of the rare times that Rae had seen Eve speechless, and Rae was enjoying it.

"Eve. Do you remember Kane?"

Eve shook her head as if Rae had knocked her out of a daydream. "I remember Kane. How are you?"

"Good. How about you?"

"Great."

The two just looked at one another as Liv walked up and got everyone's attention. "So...do we think we can get the rest of Rae's things into the U-Haul?"

Flint stepped forward. "Let me double-check."

"I'll go up with you." Rae figured this was the perfect time to talk to him about how she felt about him taking control of her move.

The two walked up the stairs and entered the apartment. As Flint started walking around, Rae gently grabbed his arm and said, "Hey, I appreciate what you did today, but I would also appreciate it if you would run things by me before you act. Especially when it's something that I am working on and directly affects me."

Flint didn't respond right away, and she could tell that she had taken him by surprise.

"I'm sorry. I didn't mean to do that. I just wanted to make sure that you could move today."

"I'll also pay for the alcohol and food for everyone for later."

"No, I got it. I shouldn't have announced that without asking you first."

Rae thought about her response for a second and then said, "How about we split it then? I'm saving money by the movers not showing up."

"You have yourself a deal." Flint stuck his hand out, and Rae stared at it before placing her hand in his. It was the second time that day she zeroed in on the sensation that touching his hand brought her. The warmth she felt from his hand sent shivers up her spine. She smiled at their hands before softly removing hers from his grasp. When she looked up, she saw that his eyes hadn't moved from hers.

"We should probably get going and take inventory to see if we can make this move in one trip."

Flint nodded and they looked in every room to evaluate what items they had left. They determined that they could probably fit everything in one go. If there were one or two items left behind, Rae could make the trip back by herself with her car if necessary.

With that, Flint and Rae went back downstairs to their friends to tell them the plan to finish moving Rae's things out of the apartment.

The group moved as fast as they could to move Rae's things into her new apartment in Arlington. The sun was setting, proceeding to cast a warm glow over her new apartment. It would have been a romantic evening if Rae had had someone with which to share the view. That was when her gaze shifted to Flint before she looked away.

The group was sitting among the boxes and furniture as they enjoyed the pizza and beer that Flint and Rae ordered.

Rae couldn't believe the number of people in her apartment. Her eyes darted around the room until they reached Flint. He was talking to one of his guy friends and Kane. Rae allowed her mind to wander as she thought more about Flint being back in her life. Why did he pull all the stops he did today to help her move? Why did he want to help her move to in the first place? Should she get drinks with him?

As she struggled to find the answers to these burning questions, her gaze moved from Flint until it landed on Eve, who was looking back at her. Rae sighed when she realized Eve had caught her staring at Flint. She raised an eyebrow at Rae but said nothing. Rae took the opportunity to walk over to Eve.

"You didn't just catch me staring at Flint," Rae whispered.

"Oh, I'm sure I didn't, but I'll change the subject just in case anyone can hear us talking. This place is beautiful, Rae. It somewhat reminds me of the apartment you rented with...

what's her name? Back when we started going to The Green Hat."

"Sarah."

Eve snapped her fingers. "That's right. Have you talked to her at all since you all moved out?"

"Not really. Maybe a text here or there, but that's it. Last I heard Sarah moved back home, but I'm not sure why. Let me go see if anyone else needs anything. I'll be right back."

The group stayed for a little while longer before one of Flint's friends checked the time and announced he had to leave. That led the rest of the group to leave the apartment. Rae stood near the front door and thanked her guests as they were leaving her home.

"So I'll see you around?"

Rae turned and noticed that the person wasn't talking to her. It was Kane, and he had his eyes trained on Eve. She noticed they had spoken some during their time together, but it had been nothing to write home about. Until now.

"Uh, sure," Eve said, and he gave a small wave as he left the apartment. When Eve turned around, Rae was standing there, welcoming her with an eyebrow raise of her own. Eve shook her head as she moved past Rae, which led Rae to smile to herself. She would talk to Eve about that later.

A few moments later, Rae realized that it was just she and Flint still in her apartment. He was busy cleaning up the trash that remained after the gathering as Rae was closing the front door. When she turned around to head to the kitchen, she came face-to-face with Flint, his blue eyes still sparkling even though he looked tired from the long day.

"Hey."

Flint smiled and said, "I wanted to say that me helping

you today was not a quid pro quo for you to go out to drinks with me."

"Did you just say quid pro quo?"

Flint cleared his throat before replying, "I didn't even realize I was going to say it until it came out."

Rae fought against the urge to giggle but lost. "Don't worry. I don't think of it like that. I'll let you know if Saturday still works when we get closer to the day. Once again, thanks for helping spearhead the move. It more than likely wouldn't have happened without you. And then you're cleaning up. That's so nice of you."

"Don't mention it. I'll take that since it isn't a no to meeting up again. I'll see you around, Rae." He stared into her eyes for a couple of seconds more before leaving her apartment after giving her a small wave.

Rae locked the door behind him and walked over to her couch to sit down. She took a deep breath as she looked around at all the work she still had to do before her apartment would become her home. She stretched to shake off some of the tiredness she was feeling and started working on unpacking her things.

Her vision for her apartment was to be traditional. Rae found that a lot of things she had in her old apartment weren't what she wanted, and she could donate them to charity. But one thing she knew she wanted to keep was the photos she had packed at the very top of a box labeled "Living Room."

Using a box cutter to cut the tape, Rae opened the box and pulled out the photo frames that were hanging in her old living room. As she was setting them up, she noticed a small piece of paper sticking out of another frame. She took it apart and removed the photo of her in Rome and found an old photo of her and Flint back when he was in the Air Force. Rae traced the happy couple in the photo and reminisced about when they took this picture when she visited him in Colorado. She put the photo in her back pocket and placed the photo of her back in the frame, in its proper place.

The picture forced her to remember the text message she had received earlier that day. Looked like whoever was stalking her the first time she dated Flint was back and raring to go.

RAE DIDN'T NOTICE the car that was idling outside of her house. It had been there for hours but was undetected by the people going in and out of her apartment. The person was taking extensive notes about what they had seen but knew they could have taken better notes if they had better visual access available to them like it was at her old apartment. She didn't see the same person sending a message to another person about what they just saw. She didn't see the person leave either once they had the evidence they came to gather.

9

———

Rae smiled as she entered her apartment. She had been working hard over the past few days to make her apartment homier and had big plans to pick up a few items that she needed to achieve that goal. The pale blue and cream furniture and décor items that she purchased would fit right in at home with the aesthetic she wanted. This redesign effort was going great.

She pulled her phone out of her pocket and sat down on her couch. There was a text notification on her screen.

Flint: Are you still available for drinks for tomorrow evening? I'm also free Sunday late afternoon?

Rae: Tomorrow evening sounds great. There's a bar a few blocks away from my apartment.

Flint: Sounds good. Just send me the name, and I'll see you then.

Rae closed her eyes as she processed what she had just done. What can of worms was she opening by meeting up with Flint?

The next morning, she cursed herself for having been up

for several hours before she needed to be. Finding that she couldn't fall back to sleep, Rae struggled to get out of bed and clear her mind. She stared at her closet before realizing there was no way in the world she could do this without either getting more sleep or having a cup of coffee. She chose the former, walked over to close her blackout curtains that she had left open last night, and hopped back into bed and fell back to sleep.

"What should I wear to this 'outing'?" Rae asked herself as she looked through her closet. She felt more like herself after getting a few more hours of sleep and showering some of her worries away. Nothing in her closet seemed right. Although it was early fall, DC was experiencing a heatwave that led her to keep gravitating toward a black maxi dress and sandals. Figuring that this wouldn't get any better, she placed the maxi dress on her bed and grabbed a denim jacket just in case she got cold while out and about.

Rae tied her hair into a ponytail and chose a more natural look for her makeup. She plucked the black satchel bag off of one of the purse hooks she had put up in her bedroom just a few days before. Since it was the purse Rae used yesterday, she knew it had everything she'd need for tonight. She grabbed her sunglasses from her coffee table and headed to the front door. Surveying the room before closing her door, she knew she had what she needed and locked the door. She tried to tame the butterflies in her stomach as she wandered toward the bar where she was to meet the one who let her get away.

When Rae reached the front door of the bar, her nerves were going haywire. During the walkover, she had tried to calm herself down by thinking of anything but this. That had all changed as she stood in front of the door. Although she didn't think anyone could read her feelings on her face, the small tremor in her hands would give her away. Was this it? Would she get the answers to the questions that had been on her mind for so long? Was she prepared to receive those answers?

As Rae opened the bar's door, her eyes locked on Flint, who was looking at his phone while he waited for her arrival, she assumed. He was sitting closer to the back of the bar, giving her some time to analyze him before she reached the table. His navy-blue T-shirt and gray shorts with black sneakers gave off a similar vibe to what she was wearing. He brushed the longer strands of his hair off of his forehead.

She took some time looking around the bar and noticed the strong character it had. The bar had a heavy focus on famous writers, including Ernest Hemingway, Jane Austen, and William Shakespeare. It had taken great care in being able to incorporate many writers into the theme and décor of the space without making it look gaudy. Rae figured this location would serve as a perfect backdrop for a writer to spin their tale together while also serving as a source of inspiration.

Rae took her time walking up to Flint. The closer she got to him, the more things she noticed. She could see his leg bouncing up and down, and one of his hands found its way to the back of his neck and rubbed it. Maybe he was just as nervous she was. When she was a few feet away, he looked up, and she saw a smile take over his lips.

"I'm glad you could make it."

"I'm never one to turn down drinks," Rae said as she sat down in her seat. She didn't realize that Flint had stepped behind her and was pushing her chair in toward the table until she felt herself moving.

"How are you doing?"

Rae was happy he didn't jump right into the reason he wanted to ask her out for drinks. She welcomed the warm-up to their conversation.

"Pretty well. Still recovering from the move, but I can't complain, you know?"

"I'm glad."

"I realized I never finished talking to you about what you did after we broke up. So spill."

"I left the Air Force about seven years ago, during which I got my master's. After that, I went to law school and ended up in Chicago for a while. I joined a law firm out there before I moved on and joined the same firm my father works for here."

"That's great. You did always say that you wanted to end up back home someday."

"That I did. For various reasons."

She sensed there was an underlying meaning to that but was afraid to know that answer.

Flint continued, "Honestly, it took me about six to eight months before I even felt as if I wasn't treading water to keep up with the workload. Things have gotten better now."

"That's good to hear." Rae leaned over to grab a menu as Flint shook his head.

"I'm an idiot. Here I am, throwing these questions at you

without even asking if you were thirsty or hungry. What would you like?"

"Don't worry about it. I'd like a glass of red wine," Rae said, studying him. "So, do you come to this bar often?"

Flint shook his head and said, "I've been here a few times but wouldn't say I come often. How is everything going with the new apartment?"

Of course, his job and apartment were in the same area as hers. Which gave them more opportunities to bump into each other outside of work. She was waiting for further instruction from him about what she could do to help him work-wise.

"Great! I love the apartment itself, and the area is fantastic. My commute time is way shorter than it used to be, which has been such a relief. Plus, it has a tub, which I've been excited to use. Thanks again for helping me move."

"I'm happy to have helped." The duo smiled at the server who approached their table and took their drink orders. When he left, Rae fiddled with her phone that was lying on the table to her right. Only a brief thank-you to their server when he returned with their drinks interrupted the silence at the table. Once the server hurried away, the silence was back in place.

"Well, are you—" Rae almost filled the silence with a question, but relief flowed through her veins when she stopped herself. Almost asking him if he was dating someone was not in the cards. Now she needed to figure out how she would cover up that almost blunder.

"Am I what?"

"Are you going to tell me why you wanted to grab drinks

together?" Rae took a deep breath after her quicksave to stop her racing heart.

The silence that surrounded the two of them made Rae tenser than she was when she entered the bar. She grabbed her glass of wine and took a sip.

"After all these years, you still can't tell me."

"It's not like that."

Rae slammed the glass of red wine down on the table a little harder than necessary. The wine swirled around, thankfully not flowing over the edge of the wineglass. The commotion was enough to force Flint's attention on her, but not enough to get him to talk.

"This is a waste of time if you won't say anything."

That comment didn't nudge things along either as Flint diverted his eyes as Rae stared him down. Enough was enough. She grabbed her purse, pulled out a twenty, and placed it on the table. She stood up and gathered her things.

"I stopped talking to you because I was trying to protect you."

Those words weren't what Rae was expecting to flow from Flint's lips.

"What do you mean trying to protect me?" She sat back down and put the money back in her purse.

"So do you remember when we first started dating? You received text messages from an unknown number." Rae nodded as Flint continued, "I didn't tell you this, but I started getting messages too. Around the same time you did."

Silence stretched between the two once more. Flint's hand rubbed the back of his neck. His knee was still bouncing up and down. In the time they dated, she had never seen him so nervous.

Rae gestured for him to go on, and she waited for him to reply.

"If I didn't cut off communication with you, whoever was sending the messages threatened to hurt you."

"Wait. What?!" Rae knew that the bafflement she felt had to be all over her face. She leaned forward. "And from what were you protecting me? Why are you speaking in riddles?"

Flint sighed and raked his hand through his hair. He opened and closed his mouth twice, struggling to find the right words to say. Although Rae wanted to act as if she wasn't bothered, she was.

"I'm screwing this up."

Rae swallowed the sarcastic retort on her lips. "What were you protecting me from, Flint? Is this your way of trying to get back into my life by making up lies?"

"No!" Flint's shout caused a few people dining nearby to turn around and look toward their table. She hadn't expected that reaction at all. It showed how much he had changed over the years because the Flint she knew years ago would have remained calm and collected.

"Rae, what we had was special. I never regretted a single moment we were together. I cared about you then, and I still care about you now. A lot. This is my way of trying to come clean and start over. That is if you want to."

Rae paused before asking, "What were you protecting me from, Flint?"

Flint stared down at his folded hands on the table. Her pulse quickened as she tried to figure out what to say to break the silence.

"What was it?"

Taking a deep breath, Flint said, "Someone would leak a

photo of us. Together. While we were... intimate. One condition I had to agree to was that I couldn't tell you why we needed to break up."

Rae stopped breathing. Well, it felt like she had. "This isn't what I was expecting. At all. Why are you telling me this now?"

"It's not how I wanted this to go, but this has been on my brain for years. And just seeing you again, being around you again... I had to tell you the truth and hope that you might be able to forgive me at some point."

Rae thought about everything he said before she formed her reply. "So I understand why you did what you did somewhat. But I also think you were very selfish."

Flint, taken aback. "Wait. What?"

"After all of these years, you think you can storm back into my life and declare that I was the one that got away and that everything will be fine? You didn't even have the decency to break up with me in person."

"I couldn't—"

"Oh, come on. You were old enough to know better. Even if you sent a letter a month later explaining things, it still would have been better than what you did." Rae thought for a moment as she grabbed the glass of wine. She drained the rest before placing the glass back down on the table, debating whether or not she wanted to get another drink.

"You're right."

"Hmm?"

"You're right. I knew better. I used the threat as a way to avoid doing what I should have done. I was stupid, and not a day goes by that I wish I could take it all back."

"Would you have wanted to stay together if it hadn't been

for this threat?"

Rae looked up at Flint after he didn't reply right away. He was staring at her, and when his eyes connected with hers, he said, "Yes. I know times were hard with me being thousands of miles away, but I would have done everything in my power to stay together."

His words and his stare became too much for Rae. She sighed and said, "I should probably head out."

She started gathering her things as Flint grabbed something out of his pocket. He soon had his wallet in his hands and placed some money down on the table to pay for their drinks. He then stood up and waited for Rae to make her move. Once she was standing, the two walked to the doors of the bar.

She turned to Flint and said, "Well, I can't say that this meetup wasn't eventful."

"Yeah, there were a few shocking moments." He rubbed his hand on the back of his neck.

"It was great seeing you again." She knew she was lying through her teeth, but here they were.

"It was great seeing you too."

"Well, thanks for the wine, and maybe I'll see you around."

The smile fell from his face briefly before returning. "Yeah. Maybe."

Just before she turned and walked away, she said, "By the way, the person sending the text messages is back. Sent me a message a few days ago."

Rae exited the bar. She looked both ways before heading back to her apartment, missing the flash of a camera that took her photo from a car parked farther down the block.

10

———

"**E**ve. Girl. You won't believe what happened." Rae was back home in her sweats and sitting on her couch. She knew that if she wanted to tell anyone what went down today, she needed to be in comfy clothes and have alcohol. Why was she lying to herself? Alcohol, at this point, was a strong want.

"Do you want to keep talking on the phone, or does this require me to come over with a bottle of wine? 'Cause I can be there in thirty."

The thought of wine and hanging out with Eve was tempting.

"I can order sushi, and we can make it a girls' night in. 'Cause let's be real; we don't go out anymore besides happy hour anyway."

"That works. And I know this is probably super last minute, but I'll send a quick text to the group chat to see if anyone else is available to come over, if you don't mind."

"Sure. That reminds me, I should probably get around to planning my little housewarming party to celebrate the new place. This party will allow me to be social so I can maintain my friendships for another six months. You know my favorite hobby is watching trashy television with a glass of wine."

"Why are we the same person? Because that is something I would do. Anyway, let me get ready so that I can get over to your place as soon as possible. See you soon."

"Bye."

As soon as Rae hung up, her phone dinged from a new text message that she assumed was Eve asking the other girls if they could come over to Rae's new place. Jules quickly responded that she was with her mom this weekend, while Liv took a few minutes to let them know she was working. Rae placed an order at a Japanese fusion restaurant that wasn't too far away from her apartment. She tidied up the papers she had thrown on the coffee table the day before and got some wine glasses out of the cabinet. A few moments later, Rae's doorbell rang and Eve was at the door.

"I think you made it here in less than thirty minutes."

"The taxi driver was moving, and although I feared for my life, I'm happy he got me here quickly because I have to know what happened between you and Flint."

"Let's get this wine open, and I'll start storytime."

As Eve struggled to get the cork out of the wine bottle, Rae turned her television on and lowered the volume. She pulled her throw blanket across the couch so she and Eve could share it. Although during the day, the weather was still somewhat warm, the cooler temperatures at night were showing up.

"Ah, there we go!" Eve exclaimed as she poured the wine into the two glasses.

"What should we have cheers to?"

"Hmm. How about finding happiness?"

That wasn't what Rae expected Eve to say, but she went along with it. "To happiness." The women tapped their glasses together and took sips of their wine.

"Oh, that is smooth, what is that?"

"It's a red blend. Recommended to me by a high school friend. I've had it a couple of times, and sometimes it's a little too smooth."

Rae giggled and took another sip of the wine.

"So can we get down to business about this Flint stuff? What happened?!"

Just as Rae was about to tell her story, the doorbell rang for the second time.

"On one hand, that is horrible timing because I want to know what happened with Flint. On the other hand, I'm starving."

Rae snorted as she opened the door. She received the delivery and placed the food down on the coffee table. "How about we eat here?"

"Sounds like a plan." The girls swiftly organized the food to their liking and got settled. They took a few bites before Eve leaned over and grabbed Rae's arm.

"Okay, I've waited long enough. What happened?"

"Do you want a summary or want to know every painstaking detail?"

"Now, why are you asking a question you already know the answer to?"

Rae smirked as she began telling the long version of what went down with Flint. The range of emotions that appeared on Eve's face as Rae told her story was almost comical. When Rae finished, Eve said nothing at first.

"And that was the end of the bar outing."

"He told you he still cared about you?!" Eve exclaimed as she shook her head in disbelief. "To be honest, I don't know why I can't believe he said what he said. Did you tell him how you felt?"

"No, because, to be honest, I don't know how I feel."

"Understandable. As you mentioned, this was all thrown at you while this has been on Flint's mind for years."

"I can't even describe how I felt at that moment. And that's not including the thing Flint mentioned outside of the fact that he still cares about me and wants to start over."

"I hadn't even gotten to that part." Eve took a sip of her wine. "And he doesn't know the creep that was texting? This person or people had to be following you guys around since the text messages came around the time you were with Flint. If I remember correctly, you didn't get another text after you blocked the number, right?"

Rae nodded. "So as far as we know, that person is still out there. Actually, we know that for sure because I got another text message the other day."

Eve spluttered on her wine. "You did?"

She took in a nervous breath. "Yep. I received a threat again."

"I don't consider a threat light in any sense of the word."

Rae nodded. "I know, I know."

Eve took a few deep breaths for several moments. Rae assumed she was trying to gather enough control not to throttle her, but what did she know?

"You can't take this to the police, right?"

She shook her head. "Chances are they'll probably say it's

a prank or something because it's not a text message that says 'We will kill you if you don't stop seeing Flint.'"

Eve shook her head and leaned back, further sinking herself into the couch with her wineglass. "So pretty much there's nothing you can do besides block the number. Did you tell Flint?"

"I did. Just before we parted ways at the bar."

Eve sat up and leaned closer to Rae. "Wait, you didn't even allow him to respond? Even after he told you he wished he had done more for you when this started up the first time around?"

Rae shrugged as she picked up the wineglass and took another sip.

"But what about the future?"

"What do you mean, what about the future?"

Eve placed her wineglass on the table and turned to Rae. "Flint still cares about you. You don't know how you feel, so everything is up in the air."

Rae made sure her face remained neutral as she waited for Eve to continue.

"Let's say you throw your hat back into the ring and get back together. You'll have to address the elephant in the room. This person who sends you these text messages whenever Flint is in your life."

"I know."

"So, what are you going to do?"

"Who knows? I sure don't."

~

A WEEK LATER, Rae waltzed into her apartment at her usual time and hung her coat up in the hall closet. She slipped off her heels and threw her purse onto the couch before she wandered into the kitchen. She poured a glass of wine to help unwind after a long day at the office. Somehow, a bag of popcorn that she bought at the grocery store earlier that week ended up in her hand, and she headed back into the living room to snack on it while she watched some mind-numbing television.

Rae thought about what Eve said over the last week or so. She had also replayed her last interactions with Flint in her mind. Not only did she risk getting her heart broken again, but there was a potential safety risk. Yes, it was minor now, but would the issue escalate as time went on? How should she handle this if she wanted to rebuild what they once had?

That way of thinking wouldn't work. He needed to help find out who was sending these messages and how to get them to stop. And if the situation got worse, they needed to be on the same page with whatever measures needed to happen. Together.

But that was if they started dating again. What should they do if she just wanted to be friends? She knew that she wouldn't mind being his friend, but there was also the potential that that would snowball into them becoming involved again. A few years ago, she would have jumped up and gotten back together with him in a millisecond. But she was older, wiser, and more cautious now.

Her mind told her that getting to know Flint again was taking a step back. But her heart said the opportunity to start something new with him was exciting. Eve was always telling her to go with the flow and not overthink things. Here was the perfect opportunity to do just that.

Rae put her wineglass on the coffee table and reached over to the other end of the couch to grab her purse she had haphazardly thrown there when she walked through the door. While fishing around for her phone, she ended up pulling out the lip gloss that she thought she'd lost a few weeks ago and placed it in its proper pocket in her purse. Finally, retrieving her phone, she scanned her messages before she thought about what she wanted to send to Flint. Seeing that the girls were talking in the group chat, she answered them to avoid the urge to text Flint.

Liv: Are we still thinking about taking the girls' trip? I need to know as soon as possible to take time off work. There's always a chance that I won't be able to make it due to wedding season, but I'll cross my fingers extra hard for this.

Eve: I'm down.

Jules: I want to go and could make it work, depending on what dates we chose.

Liv: As if we would choose dates that you couldn't make. I'll figure out some dates that should work on my end and see if any of them line up with your calendars. I'm so excited about all of this!

Rae: Me too.

11

"I can't invite him to the housewarming party," Rae mentioned to Eve, Liv, and Jules. It was two weekends after Flint asked Rae out for drinks, and the friends got together to go to barre class. They were sitting in one corner of the room, away from the other patrons, waiting for class to begin.

"Yes, you can." Liv readjusted her sticky socks and looked at Rae. "What's wrong with inviting him to the party as another way to say thank you?"

"Oh, I can list plenty of reasons I shouldn't." Rae was staring at her feet but looked up when no one responded to her comment. Her eyes darted to each of her friends, and everyone was waiting on her to expand on her remarks.

"First, we work together." She hadn't seen him in work capacity in a while. Semantics.

"You wouldn't invite a close coworker to your housewarming?" Jules lay back on her elbows and watched Rae.

"I would, but it doesn't help that we dated and had a

shitty breakup." Rae hoped her emphasis on the cussword she just dropped was enough to dictate how she felt..

"Yeah, I get that." Rae thought it was about time that someone saw it from her side and silently thanked Eve for jumping in. "But I also see inviting him because what's the worst that could happen?" And that thanks was short-lived.

"I just don't want things to be awkward." She also didn't want to spend more time with him because she feared what she might feel while in his presence. Her gut told her she could keep it together around him, but her heart made her doubt it was possible to remain indifferent.

"He seems to want to hang out with you, so why not just take it slow and go from there? Plus, if you invite him to the party, there will be plenty of people there to either keep between you two or keep both of you distracted." Rae breathed out a sigh of relief when their teacher entered the room, and the class was about to begin. She had fifty minutes to figure out why she shouldn't invite Flint to her party.

She took the time to focus on her positioning and the teacher as she guided them through another barre class.

"Where are you, Rae?"

"Huh?" Rae said as she focused on Eve. She had been so out of it that she hadn't noticed that Eve placed her hand on her shoulder.

"Is everything okay?"

Before she answered, Rae, saw that only she, Eve, and their teacher, who seemed to be preparing for her next class, were left. Feeling the heat on her cheeks, Rae wiped down the exercise tools she used, cleaned up her area, and hurried to the lobby. Jules and Liv were waiting for them there.

"I'm sorry. I don't know what happened back there. Guess I was lost in my thoughts."

"How about a penny for them?" Jules asked. "Are you thinking about what to do about Flint?"

"That's what's always on my mind," Rae explained. "I can't help it at this point."

"When is the next time you see him again?" Rae glanced at Eve before looking forward.

"Wednesday. He might stop by the office to talk to Danielle."

"Well, that gives you four days to think it over. And we have your back no matter what you do."

That earned a smile from Rae. "Thanks. But y'all think I should, right?" She looked around and saw the other three women nodding their heads, so she shook hers. "Of course."

Liv nudged Rae and said, "Don't forget, not only are we here for you no matter what you decide, if you invite him and he comes, we'll all be there to go off on him if he tries something that you don't want. Now, if he tries something you do want, please take it to your bedroom and keep it quiet."

Jules gasped, and Rae and Eve burst out laughing. The foursome got several strange looks from people in their general vicinity, but they didn't care.

Rae couldn't keep the tears from falling from her eyes. "Liv, I needed that so very much. Thank you."

"Don't mention it." Liv winked, and the four continued their strolling down the street.

After enjoying some time with her friends, Rae walked up the stairs to her apartment and opened the door. Glancing at the clock and a package she was supposed to have mailed off two days ago, she noticed that it wasn't too late to run some errands if she got to it now. She put her bag down on the couch and heard it fall on the floor as she walked into her room. She waved it off and walked into her bathroom.

Not wanting to get her head wet, she snatched her shower cap off of the hook behind her door and hopped into the shower and washed before jumping out and getting ready for the rest of the day. Rae had already decided that although she had a car, she would walk to run her errands today because it gave her a chance to get more exercise, and Arlington could be a pain to drive around in and find parking. She redid her ponytail, threw on a red T-shirt and ripped denim jeans, and figured that her white sneakers would be the perfect finish to the outfit.

She walked into her bathroom to check out the look one more time and decided that it might be worth adding a touch of makeup. Rae put on a tinted moisturizer, mascara, and lip gloss before she walked back into the hallway.

Seeing her phone and purse on the floor, she grabbed them and threw her phone in the pocket, where she usually kept it.

"Now, where are my keys?" she asked herself as she rifled through her bag. Not finding them, she surveyed the room, but still didn't see her keys. Thinking since her bag fell on the floor, they might be under the couch, so she got down on her knees to check.

"Got ya," she whispered while sitting up. She grabbed the keys, the package, and some reusable shopping bags that she kept near her front door, placed them in her purse, and walked to her door. Thinking better of it, she snatched her black zip-up and opened the door. After locking it, Rae decided that her first stop should be the post office since it would close soon. The sun was brighter than when she had been out before, so she dug through her bag, trying to find the pair of sunglasses she swore she left in it. Rae then thanked herself for being lazy and not unpacking her bag because the glasses were still there. She placed them over her eyes and headed to the post office.

Grateful that the post office was only a few blocks from her home, she was there within fifteen minutes, which was ten minutes before it closed. There were several people already in line when she entered the facility, so she waited her turn until she handed over her package to the postal worker at the front desk. She paid her bill for postage, thanked the worker, and walked out of the post office.

The walk to the supermarket would take longer than her journey to the post office because she had to pass her apartment to get there. She pulled her headphones out of another pocket in her purse, found a playlist she liked, and let the music keep her company on her way to the supermarket.

Strolling to the corner of the block where her apartment was, she saw something flash out of the corner of her eye. Rae turned to her right but saw nothing out of the ordinary. Thinking it was strange, but figuring there was nothing she could do about it, she kept walking to the store. She reached the store in no time, found a basket, and got to work getting the groceries she needed for the week. What she didn't realize was how much she was loading the basket until it became too heavy. When she was ready to pay for her things, she rolled her eyes at herself while looking at the basket. She muttered to herself about how she should have driven her car to the supermarket because getting these groceries home would be a pain. Deciding that it wasn't worth the back pain,

Rae set the basket on the ground and proceeded to push it with her foot once she was standing in line for checkout.

As the line moved, she nudged the basket along. A tap on her shoulder almost made her jump two feet in the air. She glanced over her shoulder, and her heart leaped into her throat.

"Didn't know you liked to go grocery shopping in the middle of the day on a Saturday too."

12

_____

Flint would shop for groceries at the same time and the same store as her.

"I didn't know that either. In fact, I assumed you would just have your groceries delivered or something."

"Nope. I find grocery shopping relaxing when it's not crazy busy." Rae glanced at his shopping cart and noticed that most of the things he bought were kind of healthy. She smirked at the fact that he still drank the same beer after all of these years.

"And this is how the world knows you're a weirdo, Mr. West."

Flint chuckled and Rae placed her stuff on the conveyor belt. It didn't take long to ring up Rae's items and as she was grabbing her things, Flint's voice stopped her.

"I can help bring the bags out to your car. Just give me a second to pay for the things I bought."

"Thanks, but I didn't bring my car." Rae mentally facepalmed herself because now she knew he would insist on bringing her and the groceries home. Rookie mistake.

"I can drop you off at your house. It wouldn't be an issue."
Bingo.

"That isn't necessary." Her back said otherwise while she was holding the bags, still talking to him instead of walking back to her home.

"Seriously, it's no problem. I'm happy to take you home. Let me help you put the bags in the cart." Rae stared at his hands for a second before her back won, and they placed her bags into his cart. After that, Flint turned his attention to the cashier. She waited for him to finish paying for his things and caught the tail end of his conversation with the cashier.

"I'm sure I'll see you some other time," he said with a smile and he turned his attention to Rae. Even though she knew she had no reason nor any right to be jealous, she felt a small tinge in her bones. It wasn't something she was expecting, and she knew better than to act on it, but it caused further conflicting thoughts in her mind. She shifted her body weight as she sent a glare Flint's way.

"Are you ready to head out?" Flint asked with a small grin. Now that he smiled at her, Rae could tell the difference in his interaction with her and the cashier. This smile was more genuine versus the polite smile he had given just a few seconds before. Rae nodded her head and chastised herself as they strolled out of the store and to his car.

"Here I am," he said as he stopped the shopping cart behind a black sedan.

Rae stopped suddenly a couple of feet away. "Wow. I'm shocked you don't have a jeep or a truck."

"I used to, but figured a sedan would better suit my needs at the moment," he said as he arranged his groceries in the trunk.

He strolled around to open the passenger side door for her and then set her groceries in the back seat to not mix them up with his.

"Thanks for doing all of this," she said once he'd settled into the driver's seat.

"Don't mention it. I was hoping to talk to you anyway."

"Oh?" Rae turned toward Flint, waiting for him to continue.

"There are a couple of things I wanted to touch on. You're receiving text messages again? Since when?"

Rae nodded and said, "When you were helping me move."

Flint paused. "So either someone is watching you or me, or both of us, or they are stealing our messages."

"It sounds like it, but I hate to seem paranoid."

He glanced at her before turning his attention back to the road. "I don't think you're paranoid at all. Something is up."

"Do you have any idea who could do this?"

Flint shook his head and said, "No, but I think one option we should look into is installing some sort of security system at your apartment."

Rae whipped her head and stared at him at the mention of the term we. "We?"

"Yes. Even if you don't want to date or don't have feelings for me, I want to make sure you're safe."

"The text messages stopped once I blocked the number and didn't pick back up until we connected again."

Flint stopped at a light and turned his full attention to her. "So, it's definitely because of me."

"If I had to guess, yes." The thought of it pained Rae to admit it out loud.

"If we didn't see each other, then whoever it is would leave you alone."

All Rae could do was nod.

"I think we might have our answer, then."

Rae didn't respond right away. But when she did, she had no idea if she would regret these words later. "Why are we just giving in to their demands?"

Flint looked at her with an arched eyebrow, so she continued. "Why are we letting whoever this is win? If we want to hang out with one another, we can hang out with one another. We are adults, and whoever is doing this has no right and can kick rocks."

He considered this before saying, "You're right. I think if we're going to continue whatever it is we are doing, you should still get some sort of system that will help protect you."

Rae nodded and a few moments later, Flint was pulling his sedan behind Rae's car. He got out of the car, walked around, and opened the door for her.

"I see some things never change."

"Hmm" was the only noise Flint made as he was trying to gather her groceries out of the back seat of his car.

"You still open doors for me, drink the same beer, use the same cologne."

Flint stood up to his full height and started carrying Rae's groceries toward her apartment. She bit back what was on the tip of her tongue. She would have told him she could handle it by herself.

"My father would have some strong words if I didn't open doors for women, and I'm shocked you remember what beer I drank and what my cologne was."

Realizing she had thrown herself into a trap with no way out, she told the truth. "It's hard to forget many things about you, Flint."

She could tell he hadn't expected that response because his mouth opened once before snapping shut. He then smiled at her.

Rae opened the door for him and led him to her kitchen, where he placed her groceries down on the island.

"Seriously, thanks for all of this. I know this was out of your way, but I appreciate it."

Flint waved her off. "It was my pleasure. I'll see you around." He turned to leave her kitchen before her voice stopped him.

"Hey, I'm hosting a housewarming party in a few weeks. You're more than welcome to come if you want to. I can send you an invitation if you're interested." That didn't come out as smooth as she'd intended, but she couldn't complain that much.

Flint thought about it for a second before replying, "I would like that, thanks. I think I can make it."

"I can also order a camera or something, and maybe you can hook it up before the party?"

"That works if you want to wait that long."

Rae glanced at her front door from where she was standing in the kitchen and then looked back at him. "That should work fine. I'll make sure I always lock the doors and all that jazz for now, and we can set up the camera next weekend."

"Sounds like a plan. It was nice seeing you, Rae." His eyes never left hers.

"Likewise, Flint." With that, he left.

And Rae leaned back against her counter, wondering what had just happened between them. She couldn't shake the magnetic pull she had toward him. And she didn't want to, either.

A COUPLE OF WEEKS LATER, Rae was on her way back to her office when she was startled by her phone buzzing in her hand. She knew that anyone that could see her would see the confused look on her face and wonder what was wrong. She wasn't shocked to see a message from Flint since they had been chatting a lot recently. It was his question that puzzled her. Her fingers flowed over the letters on her phone as she typed out a reply to Flint's question.

Rae: What do you mean you want me to attend an event with you?

Flint: I want you to attend an event with me if you are free. Tonight. Please.

Rae: This isn't super last minute or anything.

She looked up at her computer clock and saw that it was 1:47 p.m. She could attend an event tonight if she wanted to, even though it was interrupting her plans to spend some quality time on her couch with Ben and Jerry.

Flint: I'm sorry. I wasn't planning on going either, but a colleague couldn't attend and had two tickets, so I jumped at the opportunity.

Rae: Why not take your dad?

Flint: Because I want you to come. Are you telling me you wouldn't want to come face-to-face with Rep. John Clarkson?

Just like that, Ben and Jerry were put on ice as she mentally prepared herself to attend this event that Flint sprung on her.

Staring at herself in the mirror in the bathroom at work, Rae felt nerves in the pit of her stomach. Why was she even going to this thing? Rae eyed the dress that she had on and knew it was perfect for the occasion, but that had just been by chance. The dark short-sleeved green dress hit just above the knee, and she'd chosen nude heels with gold jewelry to finish the outfit. Thanking her lucky stars that she wore this dress today, she refreshed her makeup, adding a touch of a dark burgundy lipstick before removing the clip that had been holding her hair up all day.

After fluffing her long brown hair one more time, she gave herself one glance over, grabbed her purse and brown jacket, and walked out of the bathroom. Once she reached the entrance to her office building, she double-checked the information Flint had given her and hailed a taxi. She was on her way to a big reception honoring former Rep. John Clarkson at the Ronald Reagan Building in downtown DC. Flint had promised he would meet her at the entrance just off of the Woodrow Wilson Plaza. As the taxi cruised along the streets of DC, weaving in and out of rush hour traffic, she checked her phone to make sure she hadn't missed anything. Seeing nothing, she texted Jules to check if she might have someone else to talk to while at this event.

Rae: Are you going to the Rep. Clarkson event tonight?
Jules: No. Are you? Since when?
Rae: Yep. As of three hours ago. Flint invited me.
Jules: ...

Jules: Interesting.

Rae: ?

Jules: Didn't know you'd be going. Let me know how it goes.

Rae squinted at her phone as if that would help her understand what Jules meant. When the taxi was a few blocks away from the Ronald Reagan Building, Rae pulled out her phone again to check her makeup.

"Well, this is as good as it will get," she muttered as the taxi pulled up outside of the building. She walked past several entrances before she reached the one where she was supposed to meet Flint. She placed her coat and purse on the conveyor belt and waited her turn to walk through the metal detectors. Once she was on the other side, she retrieved her purse, checked her coat, and started looking for Flint.

As she looked for him, Rae noted how majestic the Ronald Reagan Building was. The area of the Ronald Reagan Building and International Trade Center could hold massive events in their atrium alone. The architects designed the building like many of the federal buildings in DC with its limestone exterior, but it was considerably newer. A decent-sized stage was set up in the atrium and overlooked a sea of tables, which Rae assumed meant the event had a sit-down dinner portion of the evening at some point.

"Thanks for mentioning that to me, Flint," Rae muttered as she continued her quest to find him. He was standing near the entrance of the building, just off to the side from the metal detectors. How she made it past him without either one of them seeing each other was beyond her.

Rae couldn't help but eye Flint from afar. He must have a tailor on retainer because his suits fit him well. His navy-blue suit fit him like a glove and should be his standard uniform from now on. When he turned around, she saw he was wearing a light blue button-down and a dark green tie, which was an odd coincidence because it matched her dress. Just as she was about to make her way toward him, he looked up and beamed. It was infectious because she smiled back at him.

"There you are," he said as he stepped in to kiss her on the cheek.

"Hey yourself," she said. She adjusted her purse strap, and her eyes darted around the room, taking everything in.

"Would you like a glass of wine?"

Rae nodded and said, "Yeah, it might calm my nerves."

"Why are you nervous?"

"I don't know. It just seems like a big deal to be here. I mean it's Rep. John Clarkson. Who knows how many lives and people he's touched. There are many reasons why so many people are here to honor him."

Flint nodded and some relief surged through her bones. At least he understood what she meant. "Let's walk over to the drink table and get you a glass of wine. There also might be some appetizers you can snack on while we're over there too," he said.

Rae smiled at him as he led her over to the drink table. He handed her a glass of red wine while he grabbed a beer. She smiled at his selection and took a sip. The cabernet sauvignon swished around in her mouth before going down. She had had better.

"Flint!"

The couple turned around and eyed the person who had called Flint's name. A balding man in his fifties came up to them with a big smile on his face. He looked unkempt, but Rae attributed that to a long day at the office.

"Good job on working that Sanford case."

"Thanks, man," Flint said as he shook his hand.

"Who is this beautiful woman?"

Rae raised an eyebrow at him.

"Rae, this is Steve, my coworker. Steve, this is my...girl-friend, Rae."

Rae caught herself before her face gave her feelings away. She knew it should annoy her that he put a label on them without discussing it with her first, but she kind of liked it. Still, they should discuss this when they were alone.

"It's nice to meet you."

"Likewise." And just like that, he wasn't staring at her like a cat in heat. Maybe that's why Flint called her his girlfriend. Still, he shouldn't have felt the need to "save" her at all unless they had spoken about it first.

Rae kept a polite smile on her face during their exchange and was happy when Steve shook both of their hands and stalked off to talk to someone else.

"Well, that wasn't awkward at all."

"Sorry about that."

"What was up with that whole 'this is my girlfriend' thing?"

"Well—"

"Flint!"

"Here we go again," muttered Rae when she spun around to face whoever had called Flint. She was floored by who she saw just several feet away.

"You didn't tell me your parents would be here?!" she whispered with a big smile on her face. Memories of the times she spent with his parents floated back into her mind.

"I didn't know they would be here either. If I did, I would have warned you, believe me."

"Um, why did I need a warning to—"

"Flint, there you are. We've been looking all over for you," Gladys West said as she and her husband approached the unsuspecting couple. Rae couldn't believe this was happening.

"Been right here just about the whole time. Mom and Dad, I think you remember Rae."

Gladys looked at Rae in puzzlement before her face went blank. "Ah, yes. You two dated a few years ago. It's lovely to see you again." Gladys turned back toward her son.

Flint's father, Terrance "Terry" West, smiled at Rae and stuck his hand out to shake hers. "It's great to see you again."

"Likewise," she said as she brought her hand back to rest on her waist. She couldn't help but wonder what she was doing here.

"What are you guys doing here?" And there was Flint, asking the question of the decade.

Gladys looked at her son and grabbed his arm. "You didn't know we knew the congressman? We were invited by him personally. I swore I told you we were coming." She shook her head. "Anyway, I wanted to make sure you met some key people here tonight and to let you know that we had a seat at one of the head tables for you." She glanced at Rae. "Rae, dear. I'm sure we can add an extra chair for you. Let me find Betty—"

"That's okay, Mom. We can sit with the firm."

But Gladys wouldn't take no for an answer. "Dear, it would be better if you sat near the front. The adjustments would only take a second." And before Flint could stop her, she was walking off to find who Rae assumed to be Betty.

"You know, once your mother gets her mind set on something, it will take an act of God to change her mind."

Flint shook his head and Rae snorted. Both West men turned to her, and she felt her cheeks grow warm. She would pick now to snort. Insert mental facepalm.

Terry chuckled before he said, "Ready to meet some bigwigs?"

Flint let out a deep sigh and said, "I guess so."

Rae looked up and saw that Gladys was waving them over from another corner of the room. She pointed her out to Terry and Flint, and the three of them made their way over to Gladys.

"We'll be sitting at table three, which is almost in front of the stage." Flint placed his hand on Rae's lower back as the trio headed to their table. They found their seats and sat down for the ceremony.

And that's when things got awkward for Rae. Flint was getting pulled in so many directions that she couldn't speak to him. And when she could, they had to remain quiet because someone was talking on the stage. A few of the people that came over to speak to Flint ended up talking to her, so Rae didn't feel as lonely, but it was awkward. Rae felt a gentle hand on her shoulder, and she looked up and found eyes the same color as Flint's staring down at her.

"This is what it's going to be like, you know."

"What are you talking about?"

Gladys sighed as if impatient with Rae's question before continuing, "Flint's life. This is how it's going to be. He will stay out late at events, meeting a ton of people, and working way longer hours than ever before."

"Allow me to be blunt, but I have no idea what in the world you're talking about."

Gladys shook her head. "You'll see soon enough." She gave Rae a smile that didn't reach her eyes before she went back to her seat on the other side of her husband. Stunned, Rae turned her attention back to the stage as Rep. Clarkson walked to the podium.

13

When the event was over, Rae could have kicked her heels together and twirled around. When they exited the building, the sun had set and was casting a warm glow over the government buildings in Federal Triangle. Flint had insisted on driving her home, and the two had walked to the parking garage where his car was.

"I can't believe you drove to DC on a weekday."

"I know. I had some errands to run, so I figured, why not?"

"Yuck. But rush hour traffic sucks?" Rae shivered at the thought and was thankful it was later in the evening. She hoped it would take no time for them to get to Arlington.

Once they were seated in his car, the couple buckled their seat belts, and Flint typed Rae's address into his GPS before he started the drive.

"So, what did you think of tonight?"

Gladys's comments to Rae floated up to the front of her mind. Was this a test?

"It was fine."

Flint chuckled. "No. You and I both know it wasn't. I hardly saw you once we hit table three."

"True, but I understood that you needed to network and talk to people. It was fine."

"I'm sorry about that, by the way. I didn't expect to have my time monopolized. If I thought that was going to happen, I wouldn't have invited you."

Rae turned in her seat to look at Flint. "What do you mean you wouldn't have invited me?"

"I didn't get to spend much time with you, so it wouldn't have made sense to invite you to this event."

"What? You need to spend every waking moment with me when we're together? I was happy to go with you and support your career, even if we didn't spend as much time together as we would have liked. It was a professional event for work. I understand that you were getting pulled in multiple directions. Nothing more and nothing less." Why were they even having this conversation? Although she felt better about things since their outing, this all seemed a bit much for two people who weren't dating.

Flint was silent for a few moments, but Rae could see him tighten his grip on the steering wheel before loosening it. "I'm sorry. I wasn't trying to pick a fight."

"I know," whispered Rae as she stared out of the window. This discussion was not going how she'd expected either. Flint gently grabbed Rae's hand and squeezed it in a way she assumed further solidified his apology. She placed her other hand on top of his.

"Can we talk about something else?" Rae turned to look out the window.

"That sounds like a good idea."

Rae laughed under her breath. She saw that Flint was looking at her out of the corner of his eye.

"What did you want to talk about?"

"I'm your girlfriend?" Might as well rip the Band-Aid off at this point.

"I— Um— I couldn't think of another way to describe our relationship."

"Friendship would have sufficed." She was going to drag this out for as long as possible.

"I thought that would be weird."

"As weird as calling someone your girlfriend, who isn't?"

Flint didn't have a response for that and it took everything in Rae to not laugh out loud. "Mr. Calm and Collected" was stuttering and speechless. The rarity of this moment was big enough that it should be in the record books. Rae spoke up since Flint had added nothing else to the conversation.

"Is that something you wanted to talk about?"

"Huh?" Flint tightened his grip on the wheel as they cruised through DC.

"Did you want to talk about being exclusive?"

"Is that something you wanted to talk about?"

"Don't answer my question with a question." That earned Rae a nervous giggle.

"I would like to date you. Exclusively."

"Same. See? That wasn't so hard."

"So you just tortured me to...torture me?"

"Uh-huh."

Flint shook his head and Rae gave him a big smile.

"You do realize that we're technically 'exclusive' without having been on a proper date, right?"

Rae could see the wheels in Flint's head turning. He stole

a glance at Rae before his eyes focused back on the road. "Technically, the drink for old times' sake outing was a date."

"No, it wasn't. And do you really want to count that?"

"Good point. I'm hoping to remedy that soon, but both of our schedules have been hectic. I was hoping to take you out on Saturday or Sunday if you were free? And potentially dinner on one of the other days if you wanted to?"

"Isn't that a lot for one weekend?"

"When has that ever been a problem?

"Touché." Rae got the word out before she burst out laughing and shook her head. After all, they were picking up where they left off. "We're ridiculous. Doesn't sound like a bad idea, though."

"It doesn't sound like a bad idea? Oh, how you wound me." Rae's giggles continued at Flint's antics.

She sobered up as she thought about the next thing she wanted to ask him. "So, your mom talked to me a bit during the ceremony."

Rae noticed his hands tightened again around the steering wheel. An interesting response to bringing up his mother.

"How'd that go?"

"She said some things I wanted to talk to you about."

"Go on."

"She mentioned I should get used to you being at events like this, late into the evening and meeting and talking to all kinds of people. I'm confused about why this is an issue since you kind of do this already?" Rae yawned after she finished her question.

Flint paused for a second before he said, "Yeah, I'm not sure what she's alluding to. Getting tired over there?"

"I guess so. I hadn't realized I was until just now. I guess it has been a long day today." Rae noticed he changed the subject and thought about pressing him on it.

"That it has been. You can close your eyes if you want, and I'll wake you up when we're outside of your apartment."

"That's okay," Rae said as she yawned again.

"Are you sure about that?"

"Nope."

That earned Rae another chuckle from Flint.

"What are you up to the weekend after this one?"

Rae scrolled through her schedule in her head, hoping she wasn't forgetting anything. "I don't think I'm doing anything that weekend. Why?"

"I wanted to take you somewhere. Thought I would ask now versus last minute like this was."

This brought back memories of when he took her kayaking on the Potomac several years ago. "Are you going to tell me where?"

Rae could see Flint debating with himself in his head. "Yeah, I guess I can."

"That is preferred over here, too, thanks." Rae hated most surprises and wanted to be able to prepare for anything that Flint had planned. That fed into her type-A personality.

"I wanted to take you with me to volunteer at Homes for Vets."

"Oh, the organization you cofounded to help combat the issue of veteran homelessness."

Flint winced at her comment. "I should have mentioned something about it before, huh?"

"Yep."

"So, you read the article about me in Arlington Today."

Rae repeated her answer.

"Well, is there anything else you want to know because of the article?"

"Running for Congress, huh?"

The sudden jerk of the car caused Rae to look over at Flint. She noticed that he had slightly paled, and he'd tightened his grip on the steering wheel again.

"I am not running for Congress as of now. There isn't an open seat for me to even consider running for."

Rae let out a breath she hadn't realized she was holding. "Would you run if a seat opened up?"

Flint hesitated before responding, "I'm not sure if I'm honest."

"Huh."

"What does that mean?"

"Would you talk to me before you decided to run?"

"Answering a question with a question?"

"Touché."

"But to answer your question, I would, without a doubt, talk to you before deciding to make a run for Congress. It would affect both of our lives if we kept dating."

The "if" in his statement made Rae's heart skip a beat. Was there a doubt that they would stay together this time around? She guessed it was better to be a realist.

"That was a bit of an emphasis on if."

"Rae, it meant nothing. Please don't read into it."

To prevent another argument, Rae didn't respond. This was a conversation they could pick up at another time. But she had her reservations about him running for Congress. Would her life then be front-page news? How would this strain their relationship? Is this what his mother was alluding to at the reception? Rae had way more questions, and if she were to be honest, she wasn't sure if she was ready for the answers.

Rae and Flint pulled up to Rae's apartment, where the two sat in the car in silence.

She yawned once more. "I guess I'll see you soon?" Rae said, facing him as he turned off the car's engine. She didn't know what else to say in fear that it would lead to them nitpicking each other once more.

"Sounds good," he said. But that was it. He didn't reach for her or make motions to get out of his seat to open her door. Or ask her if she wanted to continue talking to him about the things they were debating earlier. A pit had formed in her stomach at the thought of what this might mean for them, but she tried to shrug it off. She nodded her head before unbuckling her seat belt and opening her car door.

Rae got out of the car before closing the car door. She refused to look back as she walked up the pathway to her apartment. Rae hoped she had grabbed all of her things because there was no way she was stopping to see if she had. A few seconds went by before she heard someone call her name. When she turned around, an arm flew around her back and two warm, soft lips fell on hers. Flint.

Startled by the sudden attack on her senses, Rae let Flint deepen the kiss as his tongue stroked her lips, begging for entry. When she let him in, her senses went into overdrive. Never in a million years would she have suspected that she would make out with Flint in front of her apartment like two high school teens kissing underneath the bleachers when they should have been in fourth-period chemistry. Oh, but chemistry they had. Without a doubt, they had plenty of it. But chemistry couldn't be the answer to all of their problems, could it?

14

Rae whipped into her house like a tornado and slammed the door behind her. She was running late. Very late.

Work had delayed her from getting home when she thought she would. Rae and Danielle were pulled in several directions during the workday and were in meetings for most of the day. The meetings meant the things she was supposed to do at her desk got pushed back until she could finally sit down close to the end of the day and start them. And now she was rushing around trying to prepare dinner for Flint on this supposedly quiet Friday night. Except it wasn't and everything was going wrong. She had stubbed her toe twice, running past her bed and had almost tripped when gathering ingredients for dinner. After washing her hands, she took out the veggies she knew she needed to chop and got to work.

"If I make it out of this alive, it will be a miracle," she muttered as she started prepping the ingredients. She rewashed her hands and checked her phone.

"Shit," Rae said as she looked down at herself. She had

worn simple black slacks and a white button-down shirt with her hair in a haphazard ponytail because she had been running late this morning. Rae panicked for several seconds as she tried to figure out what she should do first. She hurried back into the kitchen and continued prepping the food. While she was cutting the mushrooms, she noticed a stain on her white blouse. Rae set the knife down on the cutting board, rewashed her hands, and then examined the stain. It was dry, which told her the stain had been there for hours.

Rae threw her head back and groaned at the ceiling in frustration. To make matters worse, the doorbell rang. She stomped over to the front door, and the universe had to deliver the final nail in the coffin when she tripped over the heels she'd kicked off when she got home. She swung open the door, leveling Flint with a look, daring him to say something wrong.

"Um, hi?" She could only imagine how she looked to him. Her ponytail was crooked, her white shirt had a stain and her black slacks were wrinkled because of all the running around from meeting to meeting. And with that thought in her mind, she started laughing uncontrollably.

"How can I help? I also brought this." Flint gestured to the bottle of wine in his hand. Rae didn't answer until she could control her giggles. Nothing would remove the smile off of her face now. "Good question. Excellent question, in fact. And thanks for bringing the wine. It's needed." She looked around for where Flint could help, but everything going wrong scrambled her brain. "Once again, excellent question."

Flint chuckled as Rae let him into her apartment. He removed his sweater and his shoes before following Rae into the kitchen. She sent him a link to the recipe. "That should have all the directions you need, and I took out all the ingredients so you should be good to go. If you need anything else or want to take a break, I'll be in the shower. Just don't burn my apartment down, okay?"

That earned her another chuckle from Flint and a swat on the butt before she went to wash her stressful day away. Rae stood under the spray of water coming from her showerhead for way longer than she expected. The water's temperature was perfect, and the showerhead setting helped ease Rae's achy shoulders and back. By the time she exited the shower, the water had turned lukewarm, but she felt like a brand-new woman. She figured a nice pair of dark wash jeans, a navy T-shirt, and a yellow cardigan would be nice enough yet casual enough for a lovely dinner at home. Her bare feet missed the softness of the carpet in her bedroom as she moved to the wood floors in her hallway, living room and kitchen and made her way back to Flint.

"Something smells great in here." She could tell he had at least started cooking the steak. The smell made her stomach growl.

"It's probably the steak. I have it resting over there," Flint said as he pointed to a plate covered in silver foil. "And this is for you." Flint handed her a glass of wine, which she readily grabbed and brought the glass to her lips before stopping. "You look beautiful, and that includes both when you opened the door and when you entered this room."

Rae gave him a small smile and said, "Thank you."

"Is it weird that I've missed seeing you with your hair down?"

Rae thought about it for a moment before shaking her

head. She smiled again before announcing, "We should make a toast."

Flint thought about it for a moment before saying, "To us."

"I couldn't agree more. To us."

Two hours later, Rae and Flint were lounging on Rae's couch after finishing their meal. "Dinner was amazing. Thanks so much for taking over and cooking the majority of it," Rae said as she laid her head on Flint's shoulder.

"Cooking ALL of it." The smirk that crossed his face told her all she needed to know.

"I helped with the sauce and with the broccoli. That counts."

"True, can't forget that. You're more than welcome. You know if you ever need anything, I will try to get it for you to the best of my ability, right?"

Rae lifted her head and looked Flint in the eyes. Where was this line of conversation going?

"Well, I never really thought about it, but I guess I assumed so."

"Now, you know."

"What led to that statement?"

"Nothing. I just wanted you to know."

"Are you sure?"

"Positive."

Rae didn't respond, but his comment remained in her mind. "So, how was your day today?"

"Quiet, to be honest. Working on a few things for several clients, including WPWL. Everything is looking good with WPWL, by the way."

"Do you have any happy hours, receptions, or events to attend next week?"

Flint grabbed his phone off the coffee table and skimmed through his calendar.

"Chances are I probably do, but let me check...yep, only a couple, though."

"I'm not sure how you keep up with such a demanding schedule."

Flint took a sip from his glass of wine before answering. "To be honest, I don't know how I do it sometimes either. But when you have to do what you have to do, you just do it. I don't have to attend these events after-hours, but it looks good if I show my face, and it's another networking opportunity." His snappy tone was not appreciated. Had he thought she was trying to attack his schedule?

It wasn't what he'd said that stung a bit. It was how he'd said it that caused her to shift away from him. "I get that. I was just curious."

The two sat in silence, not sure what to say next. "I'll start cleaning up." Rae stood up, stacked their plates, and took them, her wineglass, and their utensils with her into the kitchen. She started loading the dishwasher when Flint asked if he could help her with anything. Rae shook her head as Flint placed his wineglass in the sink. She started running the water as she prepared to wash the dishes.

"Is everything okay?" Flint's hands landed on Rae's waist, and as she nodded, she could feel his breath on her neck.

"Are you sure?" This time his voice was just above a whisper and he said it directly in her ear.

"Yes."

He reached around her, turned the water off, and gently turned her to face him. He hadn't given her much room, so their noses were almost touching when she looked up into his eyes.

"I shouldn't have snapped at you like that back there. I've been...under a lot of pressure, and I took it out on you. I'm sorry."

"Do you want to talk about it?"

"I do, but not right this second."

"What do you want to talk about?"

"What I was thinking of doesn't involve talking. How about I do the dishes later and we find another way to pass the time?" Although the question seemed innocent, his dark, husky tone told another story.

"And what way is that?"

Flint startled her when he lifted her off her feet and sat her down on the kitchen counter. "What are you—"

He cut her words off when he kissed her. The kiss and its intensity took her by surprise. Rough yet passionate. She knew he was leaving nothing on the table in determining exactly where they stood. She loved being the constant that made him lose control, yet she felt safe. Loved. It brought her back to when their relationship had been pure and new. But that wasn't all. The kiss was everything she thought it would be yet so much more. She hadn't been celibate while they were apart, but none of the men she had been with could hold a candle to him. And that thought frightened her.

15

———

He pushed his way between her legs, and she welcomed him with open arms and legs. The two stayed like this, enjoying each other's kisses for several minutes before Flint bent down to pick her up.

"Whee!" Rae covered her mouth. She hadn't meant to let out that noise. Her legs went around his waist immediately.

Flint chuckled and then snorted. "At least we're even now."

"Hmm?"

"You snorted at Rep. Clarkson's event, and I snorted just now."

"Wasn't even thinking about it, to be honest."

Flint shook his head and smoothly went back to kissing her lips. He soon broke the kiss and said, "Hold that thought." When he moved, she tightened her legs around his waist, and he carried her into her bedroom. He set her down on her bed before taking a few steps back. His stare was intense and he turned Rae on as she watched the wheels turn in his head. What would he want her to do?

"Take off your jeans and then lie back on the bed." The command was gentle but stern. Rae hesitated for a second before she undid her pants and pushed them down her legs. She then walked around the side of the bed, brushing past Flint and climbing onto the bed. Once Rae was lying on her back, she patiently waited for his next move.

She could see that he was taking his time admiring her body. When she gazed down, she wasn't surprised to see that her nipples had become hard with anticipation. It might have taken him a second before he climbed up on the bed, without touching her, until they were lying face-to-face. His gaze landed on her lips, and that's when it began. The kiss he unleashed on her drove her insane. His tongue caressed her lips until she opened her mouth and let him in. Their tongues wrestled for control and the groan that Flint let out was music to Rae's ears. He seemed to enjoy this as much as she did. She confirmed this thought when his denim-covered cock brushed up against her stomach.

Any reservations she had about what they were doing flew out the window. His hands were on her, her hands were on him, and that's all that mattered. In one swift move, her bra straps traveled down her shoulders, and Flint finished the job by removing the bra from her body and flinging it across the room. She would determine its location in the morning. He trained his gaze on her breasts, making her feel self-conscious.

"You're stunning," he said as he caressed her furrowed brow. His touch and words eased her worry. She forgot what was making her feel self-conscious and lost herself in the feeling of him.

He bent down to suck on her nipples. He took one into

his mouth while he massaged the other breast. When he switched breasts, Rae's mind cleared enough to ask, "Don't you have too many clothes on?"

The question caused Flint to stop his ministrations as he leaned back and, in one fell swoop, removed his sweater. Rae sat up to unbuckle his jeans, which ended up in a pool on the floor. He kneeled back on the bed and pulled her panties down her legs. She didn't look to see because the assault that his fingers were doing distracted her. When he added his tongue to the mix, Rae nearly buckled off of the bed as she tried to make sense of the sensations he was causing her body. This is what she had been missing all of these years.

He stopped momentarily and said, "Give me a second. I have a condom in—"

"Top drawer of my nightstand." Rae gestured toward the piece of furniture that held the key to them unlocking their pleasure. When he achieved his goal, he removed his boxer briefs and slid into her until he couldn't move any further. The motion took her breath away, and all she could release was a groan as she waited for him to move. Rae's moans turned more intense the harder and deeper he pushed. The panting sounds they were both making sounded like music to Rae's ears, and when she looked to her left, she could see them both in the mirror on her dresser. The unadulterated bliss on Flint's face was everything. When he noticed it had pulled her attention, his eyes followed, and their gazes connected in the mirror. Their reflections showed that they were one, now and forever.

They both found the pleasure they were looking for and rode the wave back down to Rae's bedroom. Flint rolled over onto his side and gathered Rae as close as humanly possible.

He leaned on his left hand while his right hand followed an imaginary line up and down her right arm.

"I don't remember a time when it was that good."

"Me neither," he replied. His hand moved from Rae's arm to her cheek just before he placed a gentle peck on her lips. He kissed her forehead before leaning back on his arm.

"Did you want to stay the night?"

Flint nodded his head and said, "After all, I volunteered to do the dishes."

RAE OPENED her eyes and looked around. She felt for Flint's body, which had been there when she had gone to sleep, but it was nowhere to be found. The sheets were still warm, so she knew he hadn't been gone long. She gazed at the time and saw that only a couple of hours had passed since their rendezvous. Before she could think of what to do, she heard a noise coming from her kitchen. Maybe he was washing the dishes now? But she couldn't hear the water running. She got out of bed and threw on the first thing she could find—his sweater—and headed out into the hallway.

When she reached her bedroom door, she almost announced her presence before he said, "Mom, you know how I feel about you doing this."

Rae's eyebrows wrinkled as she felt her neck and shoulders tighten with tension. What was going on? She knew she shouldn't be eavesdropping, but she couldn't turn away.

"I know you're trying to do what's best for everyone, but this plan isn't it."

Rae couldn't figure out what Flint was referring to. She

didn't want to freak out about something when she didn't know the whole story, but based on what she could hear, she knew something was amiss.

"I know this is all a part of this plan you derived. It doesn't mean I have to like it."

Rae's eyes widened after she heard Flint's comment. Was he finally going to mention what this plan was?

"Look, Mom, I gotta go. Can we talk about this later?"

She almost stamped her foot in frustration but stayed quiet. What was Flint keeping from her? And why did it seem to be a huge deal?

Lucky for her, Rae heard Flint's part of the discussion from her bedroom, so she ducked back in there for a second before entering the hallway.

"Is everything okay?" Rae announced as she made her way to the living room. Flint was standing near her television as she sat down on the couch several feet away from him.

"Yeah, why wouldn't it be?"

"I don't know. It looks like something is wrong based on the look on your face. Plus, you're up at 11:30 p.m," she mentioned, sparing a glance over to her DVR.

"There's nothing wrong." Rae jerked her head back and glared at the harshness of his tone. "Listen, there are just a few things I need to work through that are kind of hard to speak about, but when I can, you'll be the first one I tell. It's just something I need to work out on my own for now."

The softness in his tone eased Rae's immediate reaction to defend herself against his inflammatory words. She wondered if this had anything to do with what he'd mentioned the night before, but decided not to press him on it. It was a sore subject, and she wanted to respect his desire for privacy.

"That's fine. I understand. We all have stuff we want to work through, some of it on our own. Just know that I am always here if you need me."

"Thanks."

Rae felt Flint cup her face in his hand and rub his thumb across her cheek. "This whole...issue has me on edge. I will try to figure a few things out, and then when I have a firmer grasp on what's going on, we can talk about it, okay?" He smiled as he continued to rub his finger along her cheekbone.

His smile and gentle touch would be all she needed to set her mind at ease. But not this time. Rae noticed that his smile didn't quite reach his eyes, which were now filled with worry. If he told her what was going on, maybe she could fix it.

But she took him at his word. In due time he would talk to her about it.

Rae nodded and gave him a soft smile.

RAE WAS WORKING on a policy brief a few days later when she received a call on her office phone.

"Hi, it's Rae."

"Rae, hi. It's Susan at the front desk. We have a package down here for you."

Curiosity piqued, Rae grabbed her cell phone and headed toward the elevator. Would Flint send her something at work? Smiling at the thought of it, she pressed the down button and texted him.

Rae: *Did you send a surprise to my office?*

It seemed as if the elevator took longer than usual, but when it finally arrived, she stepped on and pressed L for the lobby. She pressed the closed-door button several times, hoping it would quicken her trip, but to no avail.

The trip to the lobby didn't take long because Rae was alone in the elevator. Soon, Rae was chatting with Susan about their days and eyeing the box delivered for her. It was long and made of white cardboard. She thanked Susan for collecting the box for her, snatched it off the desk, and headed back toward the elevator. When she was by herself on the way back up to her floor, she started trying to get a feel for the box, weighing it in her hands and shaking it. It was definitely lighter than she expected.

"I wonder if there are flowers in here," she muttered to herself.

When she reached her office, she closed the door and checked her phone to see if Flint had texted her back. Seeing nothing, she set her phone on the desk. Not wanting to wait anymore, Rae placed the box next to her phone and opened it. She was thankful she remembered to close her door because she knew the gasp that flowed from her lips would have drawn attention to her.

There were flowers in there, all right. Dead roses with the thorns still attached.

"What kind of sick joke is this?"

She heard her phone vibrate on her desk and leaned over to check it.

Flint: *Sorry, I just got out of a meeting. I didn't send you anything. Should I have?*

The winky face at the end made her feel a little warm

inside, but that feeling quickly vanished when she glanced back at the dead roses sitting on her desk. She took a photo of the flowers and sent it to Flint. She jumped when her ringtone sounded because she wasn't expecting a phone call.

"Hey," Rae said, immediately knowing who it was.

"Someone sent you dead roses?"

"Yep. I wish I were joking about it, but I'm not."

"Do you have a depraved secret admirer that I don't know about?"

"If I do, I don't know about it either. It's bringing up memories of those text messages I got when we first started dating. And the one right before we went out for drinks weeks ago." As soon as the words flew out of her mouth, Rae knew that she had found the answer. She didn't get these roses until she started dating Flint again. Just like she didn't get those text messages until she began to date Flint the first time around. "Someone doesn't want us to date. But why?" She gave him the rundown of what happened when she went to pick the flowers up in the lobby.

Flint didn't answer, but he hadn't hung up.

"Hey. What are you thinking about?"

"Just trying to figure out who in my life would have sent you those. 'Cause I agree that it's related to you dating me."

"Could it be an ex? Someone who's pissed that you've moved on?"

"I don't think so. I hadn't dated anyone seriously before we started dating the first time around. After we broke up, I saw someone off and on, but she is now married with a family of her own."

Rae stood up a little taller and played with the offensive

white box on her desk. "You only dated one person somewhat seriously in the time we spent apart?"

"Yeah."

"But it's been years."

"I know. But none of the women were you."

Stunned, Rae walked over to her office chair and sunk into the seat. He hadn't dated anyone seriously since they'd broken up. She didn't know why she was shocked by this information because neither had she.

"Ditto."

Flint didn't respond. Since he had nothing to add and she wanted to stay on task, she continued. "We need to figure out who sent these to me."

"I agree. Was there a label on or inside the box?"

Rae took her time examining the box and shook her head even though Flint couldn't see her reaction. "Nothing on the box or inside of it. Which makes sense. What florist would deliver dead flowers to someone? This had to be a special delivery."

"Maybe asking the front desk if they saw who delivered the flowers might provide a lead? Other than that, I'm not sure if there's much we can do."

Rae knew he was right. If Susan didn't see who delivered the flowers, then there was the chance there might be cameras at the front doors, but she might not be able to access the footage.

"While you go do that, I'll do some digging of my own. Is the camera I set up in your apartment still working properly?"

"Yes. I check the footage every other day or so for anything suspicious, but have found nothing yet." Rae took a breath before continuing, "I'll let you know what Susan says, and if you find out anything, let me know."

"Sure. I'll talk to you soon."

"Okay, bye."

Rae hung up her phone and immediately picked up her office phone. She dialed the front desk and waited for Susan to pick up.

"Hey, Susan, thanks for picking up that package for me a few minutes ago. Did you see who delivered it?"

"Oh, it was no problem, dear. And no. I stepped away from the desk, and it was there when I came back. Why?"

"I'm trying to figure out who sent it, and there was no name on the package. Do we have cameras at the front door?"

"We do, but they haven't been working for the last week. We are waiting for the security company to come back out and finish fixing them."

Rae leaned back in her chair and closed her eyes. Just her luck.

"Thanks for your help."

"I'm sorry I couldn't be more helpful."

Rae disconnected the call. She placed her hands over her face. Did this warrant going to the police? Technically, this wasn't stalking, and it wasn't harming her. It was just a nasty prank that would now bother her for the rest of the day. She checked her cell phone but saw nothing pressing. She took the photo and sent it to her girlfriends to see if they had any ideas of what to do.

Rae: Check out what I got today.

Jules: Someone sent you dead roses? Who would do that?

Rae: Your guess is as good as mine.

Liv: Um. That's pretty fucked up.

Rae: Tell me about it.

Eve: This is taking me back to the text messages. And you got another one a few weeks ago, right?

Liv: Yeah, that was my second thought.

Rae: Yep. Looks like that person is getting a little bolder. I talked to Flint about it earlier, and he had no clue who it could be. We both agreed that it had to be someone connected to him, however, because this is not a coincidence.

Jules: Is there anything we can do to help?

Rae took a moment to calm herself down while she read Jules's text once more.

Rae: I don't think so. I'm lucky to have y'all in my life.

Liv: Yeah, you are.

Rae smirked because she could read the snark through the text message.

Rae: Hardy har har. I'm not sure what else to do.

Eve: Probably need Flint to connect the dots.

"My thoughts exactly," Rae whispered to herself. She stood up, grabbed the box, and headed out of her office. Rae smiled at a coworker as she walked passed their desk to another hallway in the building. She found the garbage and recycling room. She placed the roses in the garbage and broke down the box and put it in the recycling bin. She returned to her desk, took a deep breath, and went back to concentrating on work to finish the day out strong.

A few hours later, as Rae was walking out of her office building, her phone rang. She answered it as she hurried to the metro station.

"Hey. What's up, Flint?"

"Nothing. I was just checking in on you after the flower delivery."

"That's sweet. Did you find out anything about the flowers?"

"Not yet, but I'll let you know if I do. I'm about to grab drinks with my father and who knows how long that will take. Are you headed home or out to a happy hour with the girls?"

"Headed home. You can come over when you finish up with your dad."

"I might take you up on that. I'll let you know when I'm done." His voice dropped a few octaves, and the promise of more was laced throughout his words. It sent shivers down her spine.

"I'd like that. A lot. I'm at the metro, so I'll talk to you later." Rae waited for him to say bye before she disconnected the call.

With that, Rae entered the train station.

She browsed her phone as she waited for her train. Feeling a sense of relief when she realized the next train coming into the station was headed for Virginia, she briefly closed her eyes and took a deep breath.

Rae stretched her muscles to get a kink out of her neck, and when she opened her eyes, she noticed someone a few feet away staring at her. Refusing to be the first to look away, she tilted her head as if to say What? He gave her a small smile as the train entered the station and didn't break eye contact as he headed toward the train doors. Only when she had to get on the train did she break their stare as a crowd of people flowed onto the train. Once everyone was situated, Rae looked up again to find the man still looking at her.

16

Rae grabbed her phone out of her purse, trying to convince herself that she was overreacting. Every creak and noise she heard on the train made her jump. She was hyperaware of her surroundings and hoped people didn't realize how on edge she was. She had never been so happy to see her stop in her life. Rae pulled up the note app on her phone. She wanted to write out the man's description before she forgot.

"Five-ten or so, maybe in his mid to late sixties, brown hair mixed with gray, looked to be a white man. Average weight and build," she muttered while typing to herself. After today, she wasn't taking any chances. Could this man have been the person who delivered the dead roses to her office? Rae continued to ponder that thought as she briefly glanced in the man's general direction, hoping that she would get to her stop sooner rather than later.

When the train pulled into her station, she darted toward the train doors and noticed that the man stood up too. His small smile returned, leaving a sick feeling in her stomach.

Seconds felt like hours as she waited for the train doors to open. When they did, a new surge of adrenaline was coursing through her veins.

Her heart was pounding. As she started climbing up the escalator leading to the exit, she felt a little light-headed. Rae kept looking over her shoulder as she exited the station but couldn't see the mysterious man because of the crowd also trying to leave the station. Thinking it was best to act like she was talking to someone on the phone while she walked to her apartment, she pulled out her phone and called Flint.

"Hey, babe."

Rae smiled briefly at the sound of his voice and the nickname he gave her. His words took away her worries for a second. "Hey, yourself. What are you up to?" *Five blocks to go.*

"Out to drinks with my dad, remember? How are you doing? You sound distracted."

"Not too good. I think I'm being followed."

"Wait, huh?"

Rae sighed and rubbed her temples. She was dreading having to repeat those words. "I think I'm being followed." *Four blocks to go.*

"Where are you?"

The mild panic in Flint's voice did little to calm Rae down.

"I'm walking home from the metro."

"I'll be over in thirty minutes." *Three blocks to go.*

"Don't worry about it. I shouldn't have called I forgot you are out with your dad. I'll call my mom, and she can come over."

"No, I want to be there for you. Dad and I are just catching up, but I can postpone drinks with him."

Rae hadn't realized how much she wanted someone to come over until he said those words. She would have been pissed that anyone was telling her they were just going to bombard her without asking, but when he said it, she knew she wanted him right now. "That sounds great. Can we stay on the phone until I lock my front door?"

"Without a doubt. I'll put you on speaker, so I can continue getting ready to head over."

"I'm sorry that I disturbed you, but I was freaking out."

"You never have to worry about bothering me. I'm happy you came to me. Did you talk to your parents or your friends yet?"

Rae shook her head no before she remembered that he couldn't see her. "N-no." *Two blocks to go.*

"Okay. So tell me what happened."

"So you know the whole spiel about what happened with the dead roses at work. I left my office and headed for the metro. While I was waiting for my train to come, I looked up and noticed a guy was looking at me. And this isn't saying that people don't look at other people daily, but there was something more sinister in the way he was doing it. We were on the same platform, and as luck would have it, my train was the one he got on too. He kept staring at me, and once we reached my stop, I almost sprinted out of the train. Don't know what happened to him after that." Rae spared a glance over her shoulder but saw no one. "Do you think this is worth going to the police over?"

"I'm not sure. It wouldn't hurt calling the nonemergency number and talking to someone, but there isn't much they could do because he did nothing but look at you. And there isn't enough evidence to show that he delivered those dead roses. And even with that, the person who sent them wasn't trying to hurt you." *One block to go.*

"So, there's nothing I can do about this."

"As much as it annoys me to say this, yes. But at the very least I can stay with you tonight if that would help you feel more comfortable. We can brainstorm about what might happen and try to figure out a solution to this problem. I'd have loved to have been there when the man was looking at you and—"

"I know, I know. But that wouldn't have solved anything either. What I want to know is why? And how to stop it."

She could see her apartment building from where she was standing and the sight pushed her to walk even faster.

"Rae? Are you still there?" Rae hadn't realized she hadn't said a word in several moments because all of her focus was on getting into her apartment and closing the door.

"Yeah, sorry. I'm almost home."

Before she knew it, Rae had darted up the stairs to her building and opened the front door of her apartment. As she walked in, she turned on all the lights to make sure no one had been there. "I'm inside."

"Does everything look okay there?" He must have assumed that someone might have come to her apartment too.

"Yeah, everything looks to be how I left it. Double-checking to make sure I locked the front door." Rae checked the door before finally setting her purse on the couch. Although she usually took her shoes off at the door, she didn't care at that moment and flipped them off where she was sitting.

"Okay, I'll be over soon."

"Thanks again. Bye." She hung up and called Eve.

"What's up, girl? You never call me unless it's important."

"Are you busy?"

"Just taking a break from an article I'm drafting. Is everything okay?"

"So, I told you about the flowers today."

"Yeah. Did something else happen?"

Rae sighed and took a deep breath before she continued, "Well, after that, I think someone was following me."

Eve said nothing for several moments before asking, "Run that by me again?"

"You heard that right."

"What the hell is going on?"

Rae filled Eve in on everything that had happened and took a breath when she was done.

"Looks like I will have to hold Liv back from finding this guy. And you've never seen him before?"

"Nope. I wrote down a description of him, but I just described at least forty percent of the men in DC."

"So if I had to guess, this was an intimidation technique. The man followed you onto a train and then watched you. Maybe he was a creep and thought you were attractive. As much as it pains me to say this, I rather it had been that versus someone stalking you."

"I mean, he could have been, but who knows. He had no shame. Anyway, I don't know what this means for me."

"It means nothing. All you can do is tell the police and set up some extra safety precautions. You shouldn't stop living your life over something that hasn't been proven to be a threat. Keep doing the things you were doing before and see if this will shake itself out. Have you told your parents and Flint?"

Rae bit her lip. "Flint knows, but I'm concerned about telling my parents. My mom will flip. I never told her about the text messages from a few years ago or the one I got recently." Rae took a deep breath and said, "I think this might be connected with the flowers someone sent me today."

"And none of this mess started until you began seeing Flint again."

And there it was. The harassment hadn't started again until Flint was back in her life. And if he didn't have any answers for her, then they had to work together to figure this out because it had to stop.

Rae's phone buzzed as she pulled her shirt down over her head. After she got off the phone with Eve, she changed out of her work clothes and put some sweats on to feel more comfortable. And now Flint had arrived.

She released a breath and opened the door. There Flint stood in his dark jeans, navy blue T-shirt, and white sneakers. He had a book bag over his left shoulder and purple and white flowers in his right hand.

Rae had a sense of déjà vu as she remembered when he brought her purple and white flowers the first time around. It had been on one of their first dates together, which was a surprise that he'd planned.

"I thought you might want some real flowers to cheer you up and I remembered that you loved these."

"When did you have time to grab them?" She took the flowers and let him enter her apartment.

"I have my ways. How are you feeling?"

"Better, now that I've had a bit of time to relax. Can I get you anything?" Rae enjoyed having him in her home. It gave her a sense of ease as she watched him make himself at home in her apartment.

"That's good. But my surprise doesn't end with these flowers. I'm going to run you a bath."

"Wait. What?"

"You mentioned before that you were so happy about having a bathtub again, so I thought that would help you relax. I forgot to give you these bath bombs as a housewarming gift, but I brought them this time. I also brought wine too. A red blend that I hope is still your favorite."

Rae smiled at him and said, "It is. What do you know about bath bombs?"

"Nothing. But my twin sisters do. They recommended it as soon as I told them how excited you were to have a tub."

She chuckled. "It's good to see that you're still taking advice from them."

Flint rubbed the back of his neck with his hand and said, "Well, they have their moments when they're useful."

"I guess they do. Thank you, and please thank your sisters for me." She stood up on her tiptoes to kiss him on the cheek.

"You're welcome. I'll work on the bath, and you relax on the couch."

A few minutes later, Rae was easing her body into the bathtub. She hadn't realized how much she needed this bath until she was lying in it. Flint had set up shop on the floor of the bathroom, stretching his long legs out in front of him as he tried to get comfortable.

Rae's thoughts about the dead roses and the strange guy faded away. This bath was making her body feel warm and weightless, and she didn't want to ruin that feeling by bringing up the madness that happened today.

Closing her eyes, she brought the wineglass to her mouth and sighed. This moment was fantastic and nothing could ruin it. She opened her eyes and saw that Flint was looking at her with a soft smile on his lips.

"Why are you smiling at me?"

"I can't smile at you?"

"Don't answer my question with a question, Mr. Lawyer."

Flint chuckled before he responded, "I'm happy because you're relaxed and happy. Nothing more, nothing less."

Rae grinned before her face turned somber. "We should take some time and talk about what happened to me today."

"I agree. How about you take your time in your bath, and when you're wrapping things up in here, I'll step out and order dinner if you're hungry? Does Tex-Mex sound good?"

When Flint said "hungry," Rae's stomach let itself be known.

Laughing, Flint pulled out his phone and stood up before he sat back down. "Are you getting ready to get out of the tub now?"

Rae nodded and stood up. Flint turned around and grabbed a bright yellow towel that was hanging on her shower door bar and held it up for her. She stepped out of the tub and into his embrace, wrapping the towel around herself. She leaned up and gave him a peck on the lips before whispering, "Thank you." If Rae could stay in this moment for the rest of her life, she would, but she knew there was something that needed to be cleared up before the end of the night.

Flint asked for her order and gave her a small wave as he

left the room. As she was smoothing the lotion across her body, she wondered if she was making a big mistake. The harassment started again once Flint entered the picture, and now the stakes seemed higher.

She took her time getting ready because she caught herself thinking about the multiple ways that the conversation she needed to have with Flint could go.

17

———

Rae was settled into a comfortable spot on her couch, with food and wine, now she was ready to talk.

"I want to scan through the camera footage to see if the guy I saw today popped up anywhere near my apartment over the last few days."

Flint nodded, his mouth still filled with food. After thinking about what to do for a second, she hopped off the couch and walked into her bedroom. A few seconds later, she came out with her laptop and placed it on the coffee table. She found the website where her camera uploaded the footage.

"Now this is just a gut feeling, but something triggered whoever this was to step up their game. I'm assuming it was you spending the night here. I want to look through the footage the camera gathered a few days before that night and see if anyone was watching my house."

Flint nodded. His phone vibrated and he checked the message before setting his phone on the table.

She could hear a pin drop in the room as the two scanned the footage from Rae's camera. When they reached the day that Flint spent the night, Rae paid extra attention to what was directly in the camera's viewpoint and what might have taken place on the outskirts of the camera in the surrounding area.

"Pause it right there."

Rae stopped the video and waited to see what Flint would say.

"You can't see it clearly, but someone has been sitting in that car for at least the last hour according to the timestamp."

Rae replayed the clips he mentioned, and although they couldn't confirm that person had stayed in the car the entire time, the last several clips showed someone sitting in what looked to be a black sedan.

"It looks like it could be a man, but I don't want to make that assumption. Too bad we can't get a look at their face."

"True, but we might get an idea of how long the person sat inside their car across the street from your house."

And the two continued to watch. The person was still there after Flint had arrived. The couple wasn't able to determine when the person left because nothing triggered the camera to come on after 10:00 p.m. By the time morning broke, the car was gone.

"Well, that's a dead end."

"Kind of, I am almost willing to bet that person is the same man you saw on your way home today. I have a bit of update myself."

"I wouldn't be surprised either." She turned to look at Flint. "What's up?"

"I had Kane check to see if my phone had been hacked.

To see if that's how someone might have been getting information about us."

"What happened? Why did you ask Kane?"

"Kane has done some work with hacking and is very tech savvy. In his opinion, my phone was clean. So we should have your phone checked out if you want. We can do this weekend."

"What do you mean we can do it this weekend?"

"Did you forget we're volunteering this weekend? At Homes for Vets? The organization I cofounded with Kane?"

Rae gave him a blank stare while she tried to recall him saying this. "Oh, yeah, I'm sorry. With everything going on, I forgot."

"No worries. Can you still make it?"

"Yes, and I think I invited the girls along. Eve and Liv mentioned they could probably make it."

"Oh, this might get interesting."

"Why's that?"

"My mom just texted me and told me she was coming along to help too."

RAE SMOOTHED her hands up and down her denim-covered legs as she rode patiently in Flint's car. She couldn't stop her hands from turning clammy no matter how hard she tried.

"Nervous?"

"I guess so, but I don't know why."

"You're about to meet quite a few people for the first time, so I get being nervous," Flint said as he stopped at a red light. Flint was driving them to the Homes for Vets Foundation office to help prep for an event the organization was hosting.

"Everyone will love you," Flint said, continuing the conversation through Rae's silence.

Rae didn't even know she needed to hear those words until he said them. "Are we meeting any veterans today?"

"Potentially? I'm not sure what Kane is planning to do at the office today."

Rae gulped. She usually had no problem meeting new people, but today felt different. Her self-doubts were out in full force, and she was waving her white flag. She didn't want to embarrass Flint.

"Why do you think you will embarrass me?"

Shit. Rae hadn't meant to say it out loud. "I'm not sure, okay? If I knew, I would try to snap out of it, but I'm having a hard time doing that. Your mother is supposed to be there. Let's be real - she isn't the biggest fan of me."

Flint didn't respond until he stopped his car at a stoplight. He slightly turned to her and grabbed her hand. "I don't need to tell you this, but you are a kind, beautiful, and compassionate person. There is no need to worry. We all make mistakes, so don't feel you need to censor yourself around anyone. And my mom likes you. Plus, Eve and Liv are meeting us there, so you have nothing to worry about." With that, Flint squeezed her hand and turned around to put both hands back on the wheel. When the light turned green, he pressed his foot on the gas pedal and they were on their way once again.

Flint had found the right words to say to calm her nerves. She got the feeling that even after all of this time, Gladys couldn't care less about her based on her behavior at Rep.

Clarkson's event, but he was right that she had people in her corner.

She checked her phone to see if Eve and Liv had said anything else about coming today but saw nothing. Rae typed a message to her friends and waited for a response. Too bad Jules couldn't come because she might have been able to keep Gladys at bay.

Rae: Are you still able to make it today? I should have texted you last night, but my mind was elsewhere.

Liv: Of course! We wouldn't miss this for the world.

Rae: Apparently, Gladys is also coming today.

Liv: That's even better. I want to see Gladys up close and in person. She sounds like a potential piece of work.

"That's an understatement," Rae muttered.

"What's that?"

"Nothing. Don't worry about it."

Eve: Don't worry. I'll watch over Liv...unless Gladys says or does something she shouldn't have. Then all bets are off.

Rae: Okay, see you soon.

Flint and Rae soon arrived at a large office building in Crystal City, VA. He placed the car in park and turned to Rae.

"Everything will be fine." He then kissed her forehead and opened the driver-side door. Before Rae could react, she heard a knocking on the passenger window. She jumped and turned around to see Eve's and Liv's grinning faces.

Liv opened Rae's door, and Rae said, "That was unnecessary."

"I know, but it was a lot of fun. Hey, Flint."

Flint smiled at Liv in acknowledgment. He waved at Eve. "Ready to head upstairs?"

Everyone nodded and Flint led them into the building.

Holding the front door open for Liv, Eve, and Rae, Flint sprinted around the women to summon the elevator. The elevator came relatively quickly, and the group walked on and patiently waited until the elevator reached their floor.

"Hopefully, my mom isn't here yet."

Rae and Eve whipped their heads in Flint's direction, and Liv asked, "Should we be worried?"

"No, I'm just saying I wanted to arrive before she did. That's all."

Liv raised an eyebrow at Flint, but before any of the women could reply, the elevator doors opened, and Rae was blown away. They stepped into what looked to be a reformed workspace. The exposed brick and beams on the ceiling added some character to the space that had tables, chairs, and other decor items that were mostly neutral.

"Holy shit."

"Preaching to the choir here, Liv," said Rae as she continued to survey the location.

"I'm glad you like it," Flint said as he walked toward the doors leading into the office. "Want to check it out?" The friends nodded and followed him inside the office.

The receptionist at the front desk looked up and hurried to stand up for the group as they walked to the front desk.

"Mr. West! Welcome!"

"Ellie, please call me Flint. Mr. West is my dad."

"Sorry, M—Flint. Did you want to talk to Kane?"

"Yes, but I can find him. I wanted to introduce you to my girlfriend, Rae, and two of her best friends, Eve and Liv."

Rae winced when Ellie mentioned Kane. She had forgotten to warn Eve about him. She squinted as she turned to Eve and saw her mouth slightly agape before she caught herself and closed it.

Then Rae caught Flint's eye. He gave her a wink before turning his attention back to Ellie.

"It's nice to meet you. Can I get you any water or coffee?"

Everyone shook their heads.

"We will head into the conference room. Is my mom here yet?"

Ellie shook her head. "No, but she called and told me to have her coffee ready for her when she got here, so I assume she will be here soon."

"Of course she did. Don't worry about the coffee. I'll take care of it."

"Oh, thank you! I have a couple of things I need to wrap up before I can help in the conference room. Let me know if there's anything else I can do."

Flint waved at Ellie as he led Liv, Eve, and Rae into the conference room. She could describe the conference room as "organized chaos." The room was decorated similarly to the rest of the space with exposed brick and neutral decor and furniture. But there were piles of papers everywhere.

"Are these supposed to go in these folders over here?"

"Yes. We are preparing packets of information for staffers on the Hill. We have veterans flying in from across the country to meet with their representatives to talk about homelessness in the veteran community. Side note, there is a lobbying arm of the foundation if I forgot to mention it."

Rae, Eve, and Liv nodded along as Flint went into more detail about what they would do to help prepare the materials for the meeting. "Seriously, thank you both for coming down, especially on the weekend to help. It truly means the world." Rae and Eve smiled at Flint as Liv tied her hair in a ponytail.

"We can get started while you work on your mom's coffee."

Flint looked at Rae and replied, "Sounds like a plan. I'll be back as soon as I can. Oh, Rae, can I borrow your phone with the phone unlocked?"

When she raised an eyebrow at him, he leaned over and whispered, "Potentially hacked."

She nodded her head, took her phone out of her pocket, and disarmed the passcode. She handed it over to him, and with that, he was gone.

"Shall we?" Rae asked as she too put her hair in a ponytail and looked at the mammoth amount of materials they needed to put together.

"One second," Eve said. "Why didn't you tell me that Kane would be here?"

"Honestly, I didn't know he would be until last minute. Sorry."

"It's fine. I just don't know why I'm frazzled."

"Trust me; it happens to both of us."

Liv nodded and the three got to work.

The friends had put together thirty or so packets when someone cleared their throat at the door. Rae, Eve, and Liv looked up and were met with eyes that were very similar to Flint's.

"Hi, Mrs. West," Rae said with a small smile.

"Hello. I didn't expect you to be here." The smile dropped from Rae's face. Gladys was impeccably dressed in a nice pair of black slacks, a white blouse, and black flats.

Her hair was in a low bun with not a piece out of place.

Her comment wasn't the only surprise that Gladys had up her sleeve. It turned out that she wasn't alone.

"Cassandra, please meet Rae. She is a friend of Flint's." Rae gave Cassandra a once-over but refused to be intimidated.

She was dressed up too in a long red body con dress that showed off her curves and a pair of black heels. Her long dark hair flowed over her shoulders and she had the perfect red lipstick that made her blue eyes pop. The lip was such a beautiful shade that Rae thought about asking her what shade and brand it was. She looked fantastic, but compared to everyone else; she looked like she was going to a different event. Rae didn't dwell on it, though, because she could wear whatever she wanted.

"Friend my ass," whispered Liv, which earned her a nudge in the torso from Rae.

"What was that, dear?"

"Oh, I was just introducing myself. I'm Liv. This is Eve." She held out her hand for them to shake.

"It's nice to meet you," Gladys said as she and Cassandra took turns shaking Liv's hand. She then turned to Eve and shook her hand. It didn't go unnoticed that Cassandra didn't greet Rae. "So, we just started putting together these packets, but I'm not sure if Flint wants you on a different task." Rae mentally thanked Liv and Eve for coming along today.

"Do you know where Flint is?" Gladys didn't look at her.

"He's making your coffee, but should be back here shortly."

"Did someone say my name?" Flint greeted the room with a big smile and handed his mother her coffee. The women in the room turned at the deep timbre of his voice. Rae breathed a sigh of relief because she knew she had another barrier between her and Flint's mother.

"Cassandra. I didn't expect you to be here." Rae wanted to jump up and down as Flint addressed one elephant in the room.

"You mentioned that you needed all hands on deck, so I figured it wouldn't hurt to bring Cassandra along with me. We ran into each other while shopping, and she was eager to come help," Gladys said before sipping her coffee. Rae looked at Liv with a pointed stare to keep her from saying anything, even though she knew they were all on the same page. They were "sure" that Gladys and Cassandra ran into each other while shopping, and while she hoped Cassandra was eager to help out of the goodness of her heart, Rae's instincts told her she had ulterior motives about being here today.

"Okay. I appreciate you both coming today."

Kane stuck his head into the conference room and said, "Hey, man, I need to chat with you about a couple of things soon. Need to find Ellie first." Flint nodded before Kane continued, "Excuse my manners." He walked farther into the room and said, "It's great to see y'all again." Rae smirked when she noticed that his attention was firmly on Eve. Eve looked everywhere around the room but at him. Interesting.

"Rae, here's your phone. It looks clean to me." Rae thanked him quickly and stuck her phone back into her pocket.

He turned to Cassandra and said, "I don't think we've met. I'm Kane."

"I'm Cassandra. It's nice to meet you." She had no problem introducing herself to Kane.

The two shook hands before Gladys spoke. "It's lovely to see you, dear. Can we help with anything?"

Kane said nothing for a second. *Please find something else for them to do.*

"There might be something you can help me with, but I'll need you to follow me to my office. Cassandra can help with this too." If Rae could have jumped with glee, she would have, but she figured keeping her composure was the proper response for a twenty-nine-year-old adult.

Although she didn't want to, Rae said, "See you later" at the retreating figures as they left to go to Kane's office.

"You could cut the tension in here with a knife." Rae was sure the look she was giving Liv was doing nothing to relieve that tension. Flint glanced at her in puzzlement before turning to Rae.

"Are you okay?"

"Yeah, but I think I just proved my point."

"About what?"

"Your mother hates me."

Flint sighed and ran a hand through his brown hair. "My mom doesn't hate you."

"You weren't in here when she came in. Her glare could have body-slammed Bigfoot." She could see that Eve and Liv turned and looked at her. Rae had no problem imagining their expressions.

"True. But I think my mother would have told me at some point that she didn't like you."

"I wouldn't be so sure about that," Liv said in a singsong voice. Even though Rae wanted to roll her eyes, she knew that Liv was right. "And that's not even including Cassandra." Rae looked around the room, shaking her head.

"What about her?"

Rae thought she experienced whiplash with how fast she turned her head to look at him. He couldn't possibly be this naïve. "You think she just met your mother by chance and then dropped everything she was doing to come and volunteer at your organization specifically?"

Flint's silence told Rae everything she needed to know.

"Okay."

"Rae, d—"

"It's fine."

"I know it's not fine."

Although she wanted to finish this conversation with Flint as soon as possible, she knew she couldn't. Eve and Liv were still in the room, and this was a conversation they needed to have one on one versus in front of company. "Let's table this conversation for later."

Flint turned to Liv and Eve and asked, "Do you mind if I speak to Rae alone for a minute?"

"That is unnecessary. I said we could talk about this later."

"And I don't want this festering in both of our minds for the rest of the day."

Rae didn't realize she growled until after she heard the sound leave her lips.

"We'll gladly leave the room. Maybe Ellie needs help with something...anything." With that, Eve grabbed Liv's arm, and the two hurried out of the room and closed the door.

"Rae, talk to me. Please." Rae walked over to another table in the room and leaned on it. Her back was to Flint, and although she knew that she should face him head-on, Rae feared what she would see in his body language and his eyes.

"Flint, you know I don't want to come between you and your family. And your mother has some animosity toward me. For what reason, I have no idea. So maybe it's best if we—"

"No."

"What?" Rae asked as she looked over her shoulder. As she was saying those words, she felt as if her heart was beating out of her chest. Although Rae was saying those words, she didn't want to. But she didn't want to cause any friction between Flint and his family either.

"We aren't going to throw in the towel because we are having a disagreement. I've waited too long to get you back into my life, and I will not leave yours unless you absolutely want me to. Now talk to me. It doesn't matter what it's about, just spill the tea, as you would say."

That earned a small chuckle from Rae. "That's not exactly the correct way to use that in a sentence, but I'll give you an A for effort." She took a deep breath, rolled her shoulders back, and stood tall as she turned around. Looking Flint right in the eyes right as she was about to say this almost sent a chill down her spine, but this was what he wanted, so this was what she was going to do.

"I think your mother is trying to break us up."

18

———

"What would make you think that?"

Rae closed her eyes as she took deep breathes to calm herself down. She didn't want to snap at Flint because it wouldn't solve anything.

"Besides the information I gave you earlier, I don't think she was too thrilled with me being your date to Rep. John Clarkson's event either. In fact, I would think she hadn't expected you to show up with a date. Did you tell her we are seeing each other again?"

Flint nodded and said, "Yeah. Well, sort of." He cleared his throat and said, "I told her I wanted to pick up where we left off and that I was helping you move. So you can see how long ago it was that I mentioned it. I haven't spoken to her in a while, but my dad knew. Not sure how much he told her." That information sent the wheels in Rae's mind spinning.

"When was the last time you saw Cassandra?"

Flint took a second to think about it before he replied. "Maybe at some party that my parents threw at their home a few months back."

Rae vaguely remembered hearing about the parties the Wests threw at their home from Jules after she and Flint had broken up.

"Did you two ever date?"

"No. My sisters mentioned she might have had a crush on me years ago, but that was it."

Rae knew there was something she was missing but didn't know where to go from there.

Flint took several steps forward until he was standing in front of her. He placed his hands on her forearms. She could feel the surge of electricity from their bodies connecting. "How about this? I'll talk to my mom and tell her I find it strange that Cassandra is just now interested in the nonprofit and ask that she tell me the truth. I will also mention that I am thrilled to be with you."

She thought about his statement and figured that this seemed reasonable until further evidence surfaced to either prove or disprove her assumption. "That sounds like a good plan."

"Fantastic. Now since no one else is in here, how about we move past the arguing part and get to the make-up part?"

Rae giggled before saying, "I don't know what you're thinking as far as making up, but I'm down for a quick kiss. We need to get back to work."

"You sure I can't...entice you to do more than that?"

"I'm positive. Having sex with you has never been an issue, and the thought of potentially getting caught does add some excitement to it, but we need to finish up the tasks at hand."

Flint let out a dramatic sigh that made Rae chuckle again.

"As usual, you're right. But I will remember what you said about having sex in public."

"That was the point," teased Rae as she turned her back to him and tried to pick up where she left off.

Flint rushed out of the room to find Liv and Eve, and the three joined Rae in putting together the materials needed for the meetings that were happening on Capitol Hill the following day.

Ellie soon joined the group and they made a lot of headway in getting their work done. Rae didn't know how long they had been working until Ellie checked her phone and gasped.

"Mr.—Flint, I ordered lunch for the group about an hour ago and need to run down and grab it from the delivery driver. Is that okay?"

"How about you go and grab my mom, Kane, and Cassandra and bring them in here while I go get lunch?" Ellie nodded, and with that, both Flint and Ellie left the room.

Liv and Eve slinked over to Rae, and Eve whispered, "What is going on?"

"I wish I could explain and wrap my head around it."

"Try." Liv not letting her off the hook wasn't a shock.

"I think Gladys and Cassandra don't like me."

"That's obvious. But why?"

"Your guess is as good as mine. I feel like I'm...missing something, and it's staring me right in the face."

"Yeah. I'd get it if you had done something to Gladys or Cassandra, but you haven't. Did anything happen with Gladys when you dated Flint the first time around? Today is your first time meeting Cassandra, right?"

Rae took some time to think about it but shook her head.

"Yep. Have never seen her before in my life and Flint never brought her up. For what it's worth, Jules never did either but I don't know if they know each other. They might since they run in the same social circles."

"Maybe Gladys thinks things are more serious now, and she is feeling threatened? And maybe she is using Cassandra to shift Flint's attention."

Rae staggered at the suggestion. "That's silly. Why would she feel threatened?"

"Because you might take her baby boy away from her."

Rae gave Liv an incredulous look. "I wouldn't dream—"

"I didn't say it was rational. Just some mothers feel that way, or so I've read."

"And where are you reading these stories?"

"On Reddit."

"Liv, you live an incredible life."

"I know, I know." She took her brown hair out of her ponytail and dramatically flipped it over her shoulder. Rae burst out laughing, which led to Liv attempting to hold her laughter in but failing. Eve soon joined in, and before they knew it, all three women couldn't contain their giggles.

Tears of laughter were flowing down Rae's and Eve's faces by the time Ellie, Kane, Gladys, and Cassandra arrived back in the room. Liv's very red face was trying to hold everything together but failed.

Gladys stood in the doorway with an eyebrow raised, surveying the scene before her. "Is everything all right in here?"

Rae nodded because she'd forgotten how to use her words.

A stomach growled in the room, and everyone's attention shifted to Liv.

"Sorry, but I'm ready for lunch. Is anyone with me?"

Kane shook his head with a grin before turning for the door. "Let me see if Flint needs any help."

"No need. I have all the bags of food, and the delivery driver brought the drinks up so we should be good." Flint shuffled through the door and Kane reached out to help him place the bags on the conference room table. Eve and Rae started setting out the food while Liv and Ellie went off to fill some cups of ice and grab utensils that the store forgot to put into the bags. Neither Gladys nor Cassandra tried to help.

A few minutes later, the group was sitting at the conference room table, chowing down on a variety of sandwiches and salads.

"This food is delicious. Great choice, Flint."

That was the first time in a while that Rae heard Cassandra speak during her time volunteering at Homes for Vets.

"Thanks for the compliment, but Ellie was the one who did all the work."

Cassandra's cheeks turned slightly pink, and the rest of the table thanked Ellie for throwing the lunch together. The group continued chatting with one another as they ate their food.

When the group finished eating, Cassandra hopped up and started cleaning. Rae noticed that ever so often, she would glance at Flint and look at him longer than necessary. And that was when the puzzle pieces fell into place. Her feelings for him were still there.

Pocketing this newly gained information, Rae smiled at

something Kane said before focusing on her thoughts on the situation. She felt someone tap her foot under the table and noticed it was Eve.

Liv mouthed the words are you okay and Rae nodded her head.

~

"FLINT, do y'all need any more help? I'd love to continue volunteering here."

Flint nodded and gave her a smile as Rae's eyes twitched because she was trying not to roll them. She needed to get out of here because she was worried that her eyes would get stuck in the back of her head, given the number of times she had rolled them over the last few hours.

There were other tasks the group completed before their time at Homes for Vets was finished.

Rae gently cleared her throat and said, "I had a great time seeing this aspect of the foundation." She directed her attention to Flint, Kane, and Ellie. "Thank you for everything that you do to help veterans and other members of the community."

Ellie blushed and looked down while Kane and Flint both gave her big smiles. When she peered at Gladys, she saw something unexpected. Her face was unreadable, which was a step above what Rae expected her reaction to be: pissed. Rae stared at her for a few more seconds before turning her attention to Liv and Eve.

About an hour later, Rae, Flint, Eve, and Liv walked out to their cars and noticed that Gladys and Cassandra were still outside.

"What are they still doing here?" muttered Liv as they got closer to them.

"Your guess is as good as mine," replied Eve.

Gladys and Cassandra had exited the building at least twenty minutes before them, so what were they still doing here? Before Gladys noticed the group approaching, Rae had thought of fifty different ways they might avoid being detected. But they were useless when Gladys's gazed connected with her son's. And she wasn't done dropping bombs.

"Sweetie, would you be a dear and take Cassandra home? I have to go meet your dad for a last-minute event he's attending in DC."

"Mom, you would never drive in DC. How are you getting there? Can't Cassandra drive your car back to the house and you call a car from here? After all, we're closer to DC now than we would be if we went all the way back home first."

"Well, that is a good idea. I got so flustered I didn't even think of that."

"Bull—" Rae and Eve nudged Liv from opposite sides before she could complete that sentence.

Gladys handed her keys over to Cassandra before giving Flint another kiss goodbye on the cheek.

Rae, Liv, Eve, and Flint walked over to Flint's sedan, and Liv and Eve each gave Rae a big hug.

"Thanks for coming."

"Thanks for inviting us," Eve said.

Rae stared at Liv for a second before she said, "Whatever it is you're thinking of doing, don't do it."

Liv took a slight step back with her mouth agape. "What? What would I possibly do?"

"I don't know what you have up your sleeve, but I can see the twinkle in your eye. Don't do it."

"What sucks is that I rode down with her, so whatever mess she gets in, I have to go along with it." The pained look on Eve's face made Rae chuckle.

"I won't do anything weird. You have my word."

Rae moved out of the way as Flint circled his car to open the door for her. "I know you just sidestepped what I said." Rae sighed. "Be careful."

"I always am. Now go have fun with your man."

And with that, Rae got into the car, and Flint walked around to get into the driver's seat. They both buckled their seat belts and Flint pulled out of the parking lot.

"What was Liv talking about?"

"No clue. But I'm sure Liv will report back to us in about an hour."

RAE AND FLINT were cooking in his kitchen when something came across her phone screen.

"Can you check my phone? I saw it light up, but I can't get to it."

Flint nodded and checked the message. "It's from Liv."

"Okay, give me a second." She hurried over to the sink to wash her hands. She dried them on a kitchen towel and Flint handed her the phone.

Liv: Admit that I am amazing.

Rae: Can't do that when I don't know what makes you amazing.

Eve: Even I have to admit she is.

Liv: *I can't just be amazing because I am me?*

Rae smirked as she typed her response.

Rae: *No.*

A second later, Rae's phone rang.

"Hey, Liv."

"You know your words cut deep, right? Eve is still here."

"Hey, girl."

Rae laughed before saying, "Hey yourself. Now, what are you talking about?"

"Admit that I'm amazing."

"Will it get you to tell me this story?"

"Yes."

"You're amazing. Now spill it." Rae glanced at Flint before chuckling. Flint snuck up behind Rae to embrace her and laid a small kiss on her neck.

"Wait, I'm basking in the glory of that compliment." Rae didn't reply during the moment of silence. She then asked, "So you know how we volunteered today?"

"Yes, I was there." Rae shook her head.

"And when we left the building, we saw Gladys and Cassandra outside."

"Right." Rae placed the phone on the counter and turned on the speaker. "Liv, you're on speaker. Figured Flint would want to hear this too." She then moved to place a lid on the pot.

"Oh, I'm sorry. Did we interrupt anything?"

"Only us making dinner. Get your mind out of the gutter."

"But that's its permanent residence. Anyway, when you guys left, Eve and I stayed for a bit longer. I hoped it came across as us trying to fix my GPS or something. When I pulled away, they were still there, and I figured that it doesn't take that long to call a car in Crystal City."

"Right."

"I pulled out of the parking spot and made a U-turn and parked my car down the street where I still could see inside of the parking lot. And then we waited."

"I think it was maybe twenty minutes?" Eve chimed in with her recollection.

Rae recognized Liv's pause for dramatic effect.

"You guys aren't any fun. Anyway, Gladys and Cassandra left together. Gladys was driving."

Rae's eyes widened and she turned to look over her shoulder at Flint. He gently broke the embrace and took his phone out of his pocket. He didn't say a word.

Rae took the time to choose her words carefully because Gladys was still Flint's mother.

"Does this mean that either Gladys took Cassandra home and then came back to attend the event in DC, or she just went home and didn't go anywhere?"

"I don't know, but that would have been taking her farther out of her way."

Rae took another glance at Flint, trying to figure out what he was thinking. His furrowed brows and the stare he gave his phone was without a doubt cause for concern. Had he found something else out?

"Okay, Nancy Drew and George Fayne. I will let you both go, but thanks for the update. This information is probably a piece to the large puzzle at hand."

"Don't mention it. And I'm Nancy, Eve. Talk to you soon." And with that, Liv and Eve hung up.

No one spoke for several seconds. Rae was over the

silence and asked, "Hey, did you find anything suspicious on my phone that would show that it was being hacked?"

"No. Doesn't mean there aren't other ways to hack it, however." His response was curt and his attention was stuck on his phone.

"What's wrong?"

Flint didn't answer. He showed her his phone and she read the messages.

Flint: Hey, Dad. What are you doing?

Dad: Heading into DC for an event. Is everything okay?

Flint: Yep. I was just curious and was thinking about coming over.

Dad: Oh great! I should be home in a few hours.

"Huh. I don't mean this as any disrespect, but that doesn't mean your mom was with your dad."

"True. But a lot of this is circumstantial."

"Also true. My intention is not to accuse her, but she brought Cassandra to the foundation without telling you beforehand..."

Flint nodded. "We can't do anything with that evidence, so we should drop it for now."

But Rae knew that this was far from over.

19

Several weeks later, Flint invited Rae over to his apartment for the first time after a night out on the town.

"Nice place you have here." Rae examined the layout of his apartment. She concluded that he had to be paying a small fortune to live here. Between the doorman at the front door, the beautiful views of the city, the amount of space in the apartment, his rent had to be way higher. While she looked over the stainless-steel appliances and white and gray countertops, she was in complete awe that he had this much kitchen space in his apartment compared to hers.

"Please tell me you cook a ton in here. It would literally be a sin if you didn't."

Flint tittered and said, "I cook here and there, but was hoping to learn more at some point. One of my potential date ideas was to do a cooking class with you."

That snapped Rae out of her daydream about cooking in Flint's kitchen. "Really? That sounds like a lot of fun."

"I thought it might be something fun and out of the box.

You used to like when our dates were not your standard dinner and a movie type." Flint's gaze landed on Rae as he walked over to her and gently grabbed her hand.

Rae's thoughts floated back to the time when he surprised her with a kayaking date down the Potomac River. It had been something that she'd always wanted to do, and his ability to do his research impressed her. She also liked that he kept her on her toes from that date until their relationship ended.

With that sobering thought, she shifted her body from his and swallowed hard. She clutched her stomach as she took a few steps away from him, under the guise of looking around his apartment. Rae hoped it was enough for him not to notice how hurt she still was by their separation.

"Rae."

She turned back to look at him and was startled by the look in his eyes. There was a sense of vulnerability.

Flint cleared his throat before saying, "My one regret is losing what we had. I regret losing you."

If she'd dropped a pin, the sound would have echoed throughout the walls of the apartment.

"You do?" Rae wanted to slap herself for displaying the uncertainty that she felt. She shook the feeling off and stared right into his eyes.

"Yes."

"Then why did you think it was okay to do what you did?"

"It's not that I thought it was okay... Well, I guess I did because I did it, huh?"

Rae nodded but said nothing else. Her eyes didn't waver.

"I shouldn't have ignored you like I did."

"Ghosted was more like it."

Flint rubbed the back of his neck and looked down. Her gaze remained unchanged as he shifted his body weight and peered back at her.

"To be honest, there was more to it than just the threats. I was scared."

"Scared of what?"

Flint shifted his body weight once more and paced. "I was scared of where we were going. We were both so young, and things were serious for lack of a better word. And I knew then, I wasn't the right person for you."

"And what about now?"

"I hope to prove that I am the right person for you." He pulled her into his embrace and held her. Bending down, he took a moment to brush his lips over Rae's hair. The caring gesture was her undoing. She stood on her tiptoes and pressed her lips to his. The kiss started softly before it grew bold and hungry. Clothes were flying off body parts. If Rae had had time to think about it, it would have annoyed her that once again, she would have to go on a hunting expedition for her clothes. To make matters worse, they had gone to Flint's apartment, so she hoped the clothes that were tossed remained in plain sight. Rae smiled as she backed Flint up toward his couch and pushed him down onto it.

"Have you ever had sex on this couch?" Flint answered with a shake of his head. "Good." Her lips descended on his once again.

"You know, I can get used to this view. You on top," said Flint as his hand roamed up her body. The loud laugh Rae let out would have left her self-conscious in any other situation. But here she felt she could be herself. Unapologetically her.

She didn't understand how he flipped them as smoothly

as he did because all that was on her mind was him filling her up. Inch by inch. He painstakingly took her, giving all of himself. She didn't know what made this time feel so different, but it did. And the thought scared her.

RAE COULD FEEL Flint's eyes on her. She assumed that he thought she was sleeping and she very well should have been. Rae dozed off after they made their way to his bed, but his light, feather touches on her bare back had woken her up. She let him continue tracing imaginary lines before she flipped over to lie on her side. The gentle smile on her face seemed to relax the lines on his forehead he tried to hide from her when she got a good look at his face in the moonlight.

"Why are you still awake?"

"Just thinking. I wanted to talk to you about something."

Carefully, Rae sat up, pulling the covers over her naked body. What could he possibly be thinking about this late at night? She mentally prepared for the worst.

He gently grabbed her hand and held it between both of his. Rae's mind raced because she sensed how important this topic was to him.

"So, I've been thinking about running for office."

Rae's face remained blank as she tried to process what he was saying. "Run for office of what?"

Flint chuckled before replying, "I'm eighty-five percent sure I want to run for Congress."

"You're kidding. You really want to do it?"

"I'm not, and I do. I also wanted to tell you Rep. Clarkson

is retiring."

"Wow. Wait. What?! How did you find that out?" Flint wanting to run for Congress wasn't shocking because he has tossed the idea out before. Rep. Clarkson wanting to retire was a whole different discussion.

"Now, my running hasn't been decided, but it's something I've debated for a while, as you know. I wanted to see what you thought about it. And Rep. Clarkson retiring hasn't officially been announced, but that's what he's apparently telling some of his closest friends. Which includes my parents, which is how I found out."

"Ah, I'm not sure what to think about it. I wasn't expecting any of this."

"I'm sorry. It was something I promised I would talk to you about before I decided. I'm hoping this is something we can do together."

Rae said nothing for several moments. "I'm not sure what to say." She paused again. "I know how much your foundation means to you. Would you still be able to be a part of it if you ran and won?"

"Haven't exactly figured all of that out, but I know we'll make something work. And this is all if I run. That isn't set in stone."

"But you definitely want to."

Flint nodded. "My heart says yes, but my brain knows how much more difficult this will be on the people I love and on me." He focused his eyes on her. "When I think of my future, I see you in it. Your opinion on all of this means a lot to me. The decision to run for office will affect us as individuals and as a couple."

It took everything in Rae not to swoon and cry at the

same time. Swoon that he saw a future with her. Cry at how this might change their relationship.

"I'm glad you think that way. I want to be there as you achieve your dreams, so if you throw your hat in the ring, I want to support you. I think we should continue to talk it over, however."

Flint smiled and said, "That makes sense."

"Could you talk more about how you think your campaigning will affect us?"

"Well, if I run and we continue to date, then that might open your life to scrutiny. Now I would run for a congressional seat, so chances are it won't attract as much media attention as say, a Senate race, but who knows. That's beside the long hours that will be spent on the campaign trail. Our free time and dates would be harder to come by."

Rae shook her head at Flint. "Maybe Eve would be put on your beat. In terms of us, we will figure out how to make it work."

Flint smiled at the thought. "Maybe, but it might be a conflict of interest even though I think she would be fair versus trying to paint me in the best light possible. And I know we will."

"Anyway. This decision is a lot to think about. When do you need to decide, and I assume submit paperwork?"

"In a few months. I've been toying with the idea for a bit because my parents heard Rep. Clarkson might be retiring to spend more time with his family, but wasn't seriously considering it until the last couple of days."

"No matter what you do, I'll still be proud of you."

Flint leaned over, took Rae into his arms, and gave her a sensual kiss.

20

"Girls, I can't shake it."

Rae looked around the table to see three pairs of eyes staring back at her.

"Flint's mother is up to something, and I know it. But what exactly? No idea."

"Yeah, and it's not like you can go up to her or Flint and make the case based on a feeling. It's his mother. But I agree with you. Something is...off." Eve finished her comment by stuffing a pretzel bite in her mouth.

The Green Hat was quieter than usual and Rae preferred it that way. A lot was on her mind, and the quieter atmosphere of the bar gave her a chance to think.

"I still stand by what I said happened a few weeks ago," Liv said before grabbing her phone. "Her plan to get Flint to take Cassandra home backfired."

"And I completely believe you. Honestly, I think Gladys wanted Flint to take Cassandra and probably wanted you to drive me."

Liv sat up, straighter in her chair. "I thought the same

thing but didn't want to say it out loud. Which is unusual for me?"

"What would be the point in that, though?" Jules chimed in with her question before taking a sip of her water.

A thought popped into Rae's head. "Wait, Jules. I assume you know at least something about Cassandra. What can you tell us about her?"

"I don't know her all that well, just that her parents run in the same circles as the Wests. Her father is the CEO of a company that I can't remember the name of at the moment, and I think her mom is a socialite? I have heard little about her other than she attends events with her husband. I don't understand why Mrs. West would have been hanging out with Cassandra without her mother, but I would assume that she and Mrs. Hopkins are at least associates. I can probably find out more. My mom doesn't particularly like her, but I am sure she's heard something."

"Do you know if Cassandra's our age or younger? I'm wondering if she might have been friends with Flint's younger siblings because at least according to him, he doesn't really know her all that well, and she never took an interest in his foundation until now."

"I might find that out. I know that Flint's sisters knew of her, and that's how I heard of her. It's weird for Mrs. West and Cassandra to hang out or come to Homes for Vets without Mrs. Hopkins being involved in the meeting's planning."

Strange, thought Rae as she polished off her beer.

"Has Flint said anything else about what happened?" Liv asked.

Rae shook her head. "Not a word. And I don't want to bring it up and potentially cause another fight. I stand by my conclusion that she doesn't like me, and something strange is happening whether Flint wants to admit it or not. I'm sure Gladys is used to getting her way, so I know she'll try again to achieve her goal." Rae cleared her throat and continued. "On to happier news, Liv, how is planning the girls' trip going?"

"Fantastic. Thanks for booking your flights. I'm putting the itinerary together and have a couple of surprises up my sleeve." Liv bounced up and down in her seat.

"I'm a little scared of what you have planned based on the look on your face," Eve said as she leaned away from Liv. Liv then stuck her tongue out at her.

"You have nothing to fear. Everything that I have planned is mostly legal."

"I bet that did nothing to ease Eve's fears," Rae said with a smirk.

"And you would be correct," Eve said as she nodded her head in agreement.

"It will be fun, don't you worry. I had Jules help me a bit, and you know she wouldn't let me do anything too crazy."

Jules looked at her and said, "Well, the things I have seen were tame, especially for Liv, but I can't vouch for the other excursions that I haven't seen." She paused for a second before she said, "I'm super excited, though. Trying to wrap everything up before we leave in a couple of weeks."

"Same, but nothing compares to the craziness I had to deal with between moving and a board meeting all in the same month. I'm glad it went well and that it's over."

"I have to give you props for doing that because I would have pulled out my hair...or grown little gray ones," Eve said as she gave Rae a high five.

Rae shrugged before saying, "Sometimes, just do what you have to do. It all worked out, and I love my apartment."

Eve leaned forward toward Rae. "Are you even staying there much? The last few times I texted you, you were at Flint's place."

"That's...not inaccurate."

Liv jumped up and whispered rather loudly, "How often are you over there?!" She looked around and noticed that she was drawing attention to herself, so she sat back down.

Rae thought about it for a moment. "At least twice a week now."

"Oh, that's not as bad as I was thinking. I would say, why don't you just move in with Flint and save a bit of money since it makes little sense to pay rent in a place you aren't staying at regularly?"

Rae drank from her water glass. "Well, he hasn't brought that up, and I enjoy having my space to come home to and to call my own for now. We'll see where the future leads." The other three women nodded before Rae continued. "He asked me out to dinner at a nice restaurant on Saturday evening that I'm excited about."

"Why?" Jules asked as she glanced down at her phone to check the time.

"Because it's at a super fancy restaurant. At least that is what my research told me."

"Is it for a special occasion?"

Rae shook her head. "Unless I'm forgetting something there isn't anything special about this upcoming weekend."

"Could it be a restaurant that he just wanted to try out?"

Rae shrugged her shoulders. "It could be, but he never mentioned it."

Liv turned to her again and grabbed her left hand. "Do you think he will propose?"

Rae's eyes almost bulged out of her face. Her mouth was agape and the words she wanted to say died on her lips. "That's a leap. And it would be a bit quick for us. Plus, I would like him to get to know my parents and see how they react to one another." Rae paused for a second. "I haven't even reintroduced them to him yet and we haven't talked about it much since getting back together. He knows that is a conversation I would like to have before we move to start on the path to making things permanent."

"Understandable," Eve said. Rae could feel her eyes on her. She knew Eve was studying her reaction to pinpoint how she felt one way or the other, but Rae kept a neutral expression on her face to mask her feelings. Knowing Eve, she could probably look past the veneer and see what she was feeling anyway.

"So anyway, enough about me. How is everyone doing?"

"Girl, just busy, and I'm sure I can speak for everyone on that front," stated Eve as everyone nodded along.

"How's everyone doing on the dating front?"

The scene before Rae ended up being comical. Eve glared at her, while Jules choked on her water, and Liv threw her head back as if someone had slapped her. Then the groans erupted.

"You know better than to speak those words around us," Liv said, her head still in the "been slapped" position. Rae's laughter was bubbling at the surface.

Rae shook her head at her friend before continuing, "I seriously don't know what I would do without you all."

"We don't know how you would survive either," Eve said

with a smirk on her face. And that was all it took. Rae's laughter flowed out like water from a ruptured dam. She hadn't laughed this hard in over a week, and she knew she needed it.

Her laughter was contagious because Jules had to place her glass of water down to keep from spilling it. She threw her hand over her mouth to help her swallow the remaining water that she had in it.

Watching Jules sent Eve into a hysterics, which led to her snorting. By that point, Liv had sat back up, but the snort sent her over the edge, and she threw her head back again and was holding her chest to stop from laughing.

Rae somewhat sobered up and wiped the tears of laughter from her eyes. She looked around the table and smiled. She knew these women would be in her corner no matter what.

21

"This restaurant is stunning."

Rae took a moment to look around to get a feel for the place. The lights were dimmed, but because of candles on the tables, it was still bright enough to see around the restaurant. She had made the right choice by wearing a black dress and heels. Jules had recommended that she wear her hair up and she had done just that. Rae placed her coat on the back of her chair and Flint pushed her seat in after she sat down. She took the opportunity to look around. The restaurant's decor was stunning, focusing on natural colors. Because of the hour they had arrived and the dimming of the lights, the room gave off a romantic vibe.

"How did you find out about this restaurant? I'm in love with it, and I haven't eaten anything yet," said Rae as Flint got situated across from her.

"I'm glad you like it. A coworker recommended it to me," Flint said as he picked up his menu. "How about we pick what we want and then go from there?"

The smile he gave her threw her somewhat off-kilter. Was

she wrong to have immediately dismissed Liv's assumption that he might want to propose? But they weren't ready for that next step yet and hadn't even talked about marriage recently.

Rae picked up the menu and studied it to stop her thoughts from racing out of control. Picking what she wanted, she sat back and waited on Flint. When he looked up, he briefly smiled at her before turning his attention to their server. The couple gave their order, and Rae waited for Flint to fill her in on what he wanted to talk about. He reached across the table and grabbed her hand, silently playing with her fingers for a bit. And with that, Rae's patience flew out the window.

"So, what's up?"

"Rae, there is something I've meant to tell you."

Flint paused but didn't continue. He squinted, trying to see something over her shoulder.

"Dad?"

Rae swung her head around and her eyes ran smack dab into Terry West.

"Hey, son."

"What are you doing here?"

Rae thought that was an excellent question and mentally gave Flint a high five for it.

"Your mom and I were having dinner, and when she went to the bathroom, I looked over and saw you were here having dinner with Rae. It's lovely to see you again," Terry said, sparing a glance at Rae.

"Likewise," Rae said. Out of all the restaurants in the DC Metropolitan Area, Flint's parents had to be dining at the one he picked out? What were the chances of that?

As Rae shifted her thoughts to the back of her mind, Gladys West strutted up to the table with a huge smile. Rae could immediately feel the tension rising in her head. The headache was already forming and she wished she could take something to keep it at bay.

"Hi, sweetie." Gladys smiled at Flint and Rae could see the love she had for her son. But when her gaze turned to Rae, she could see the shift. Not that she expected Gladys to like her nearly as much as she loved her son, but the look in her eyes didn't tell any lies.

"Did you submit the paperwork?"

Rae stared a hole into Flint's eyes as she waited for a response. She replayed Gladys's comment in her head multiple times, and each time, the glare on her face was transfixed. He had hidden something from her. What paperwork was he supposed to have turned in? When Gladys's attention shifted to her once again, she knew she had made a mistake by asking the question out loud.

"Oh, Rae, dear, you hadn't heard? Our son here has decided that he is running for Congress."

The oxygen in Rae's lungs was all but gone after Gladys's announcement.

"What is she talking about?"

"Rae, this isn't official—"

"So, you didn't turn in the paperwork today?" Gladys chimed in from the peanut gallery.

Flint ignored her. "This is what I was hoping to talk to you about tonight."

"What was there to talk about? You were already filling out the paperwork."

Flint ignored his mother again. "Rae, this a decision I want us to make together."

"Well, that isn't—"

"Mom, can you please stop?"

Rae was stunned at his response as she watched the two go back and forth like they were playing a match at the US Open. She noticed that Terry was doing the same thing, so he was in the dark about all of this. And that was when she too had decided.

"I—I think I need to go."

"Rae, wait—"

"No, I need to go." As Rae got up out of her chair, she almost knocked over her glass of water but caught it before she made too much of a mess.

"I would love to say that I had a great time, but that would be a lie. Bye, Flint. Mr. and Mrs. West," she said as she nodded in acknowledgment. She noticed the small smile on Gladys's face but honestly couldn't care less. She made motions to gather her things and Flint placed his hand over hers. Jerking her hand out of his grasp, she said, "Don't touch me."

"I guess you hadn't." Gladys had to have the last word.

"Gladys, this was unnecessary. We should be going. See you tomorrow for lunch, Flint?"

Flint nodded and watched his parents leave the restaurant. As they waved goodbye and walked away, neither Rae nor Flint said a word.

A few beats passed before Rae decided she had to speak up. "Were you going to tell me that tonight? That you were officially planning on making a run for a congressional seat?"

Flint quickly ran his hand through his hair, making it

even messier than it had been before. "Yes. First, let me correct what my mother said. I haven't made any motions to file since we talked about it last. Nothing has been signed or dated. Tonight, I planned to talk to you more about it over dinner. I want your input because I would need to decide sooner rather than later."

After she closed her eyes, she leaned back in her chair as he explained his side of the story. This decision wasn't something he was trying to hide from her. He just hadn't brought it up yet. And Gladys was once again trying to start trouble.

"What does this have to do with you? Do you want to run, or is it because your father wants you to because of his involvement in Virginian politics?"

Flint hesitated for a moment before replying, "Yes. I think I can make a difference or at least do my damnedest to make a difference. I'm more concerned about how it will affect the people I love. If I run, I know it might open up family and friends to some scrutiny if I end up gaining traction." When he said the last part, Rae noticed his pointed stare at her.

"When do you have to file?"

"Within the next few weeks. If I enter, I'm hoping to get a jump on the other candidates who might throw their hat into the race for the nomination."

"Okay. Well, we still have a little time before you decide."

"I'm just happy you at least seem open to the idea."

Rae wanted to be open to the things that Flint wanted to achieve. If it was important to him, it was important to her, and she hoped he felt the same.

But as Rae was getting into bed that night, the more she thought about it, the more of an eerie feeling she had about the whole thing that she just couldn't shake.

22

———

The sound of Rae's text notification brought her out of a daydream she was having. She was home alone a few weekends later sitting on her couch with the television on, mindlessly listening to some reality show while surfing the internet. The only light in the room was the glow emanating from her laptop and tv. She had spent most of the time alone thinking about Flint's dilemma about starting a congressional campaign but was coming up empty. Leaning over to grab her phone took more energy than Rae was willing to give at that moment, so she ignored it. When it buzzed again, she finally mustered up enough power to reach over to grab the device that was ruining her time in solitude.

Liv: Did you see the photo that had Jules was tagged in?

Eve: No. Why did you send us a separate group chat?

Rae: Nope. I'm rarely on social media nowadays, anyway.

And just like that, Rae's quiet time had been interrupted, but she was okay with it. At least she had gotten a little time to herself. She placed her laptop on to the cushion next to her and stood up. Briefly stretching to get the kinks out of her limbs after sitting for far too long, she slipped into her house shoes, grabbed her phone, and brought it with her into the kitchen. She set it down on the countertop as she looked around to find the things she needed to make a cup of tea. She grabbed a mug from her cabinet and filled it up with water before putting it into the microwave to heat. Wandering over to her pantry, she found some teas her mom had probably left the last time she visited her apartment. Saying a silent thanks, she found one that contained lemon and ginger and waited for the microwave to go off. As the timer beeped, she quickly grabbed the mug handle and placed it on the counter. She dropped the teabag into the mug and waited for it to steep.

Thinking it was weird that Liv hadn't responded to their texts, Rae's fingers flew across the keyboard to compose a message.

Rae: What happened?

As she waited for a response from Liv, and for her tea to be ready, she opened up her last text message from Flint and smiled. Realizing it had been a while since they had last spoken, she typed a text to him too.

Rae: I miss you. What are you up to?

Maybe he would come over to her apartment tonight for a quiet night in. Or heck, she didn't even mind going over to his apartment to spend time with him either. And that was saying something because she was already in her T-shirt and yoga pants. After all, she planned on staying home for the night.

A few more minutes passed before Rae realized her tea had to be ready. Just as she was about to take a sip, her text message ringer went off. Thinking nothing of it, she brought the mug to her lips as she clicked on the notification.

The cup slipped from her hand and crashed onto the wood floor.

"Shit!" Rae exclaimed as she saw the mess she'd made. She breathed a sigh of relief when she realized that none of the hot liquid had gotten on her. Silently, Rae thanked her quick reflexes as she placed her phone on the counter and bent down to pick up the bigger shards of the mug. She couldn't have seen what she thought she'd seen.

The loud ring of her phone interrupted her cleaning, and she welcomed that reprieve because she knew her thoughts were about to race.

"Hello?"

"Hey, it's Liv and Eve."

"Hey."

Rae didn't know what else to say.

"I'm so sorry." Rae could hear the sincerity in Eve's tone.

"I'm not even sure how to process what I just saw."

"Do you want us to come over?"

Rae took some time to concentrate on breathing before answering. "No. I think I'll be okay."

"You don't sound okay." Rae could hear the concern in Liv's voice.

"I think I'm still in shock. Plus, I'm trying to pick up the mug I dropped after seeing that photo."

The photo that Rae saw had Jules, Flint, and Cassandra in it. It looked to be taken at another event that Flint and Jules had attended. That didn't bother Rae. What bothered her was the fact that in the photo, Cassandra was pressed up against Flint. Her chest was firmly attached to his torso, and she couldn't see where his hand was. And Cassandra looked to be whispering something in his ear. Although she assumed there was an explanation for this, she couldn't control the rage building in her mind. Her hand trembled as she tried to listen to what her friends were telling her on the phone.

"Were there any other photos that were posted with this one?"

"I didn't even think to check because I wanted to make sure you knew about it. Hold on."

"I'm asking because, in the photo, Flint and Cassandra weren't looking at the camera. I'm curious to see if there were more photos taken where they were looking at the lens."

Rae and Eve waited in silence as Liv searched for more photos of the event.

"Ah," whispered Liv just before Rae heard her phone ping.

Rae tossed the paper towels she had been using to clean up the mess in the garbage and washed her hands. Then she checked her phone to see what Liv had sent her. There were a few more photos shot of the three. In them, Flint and Cassandra looked like a couple. One photo showed him gazing down into her eyes and smiling, another with him whispering into her ear.

"I'm getting a headache," Rae said as she studied the photos. Flint looked...happy with her. "Were these taken tonight?"

"I'm not sure, but they were posted tonight, however."

Rae could feel her anger building. "Flint was with me the night before last, so it wasn't then. And he's supposed to be at dinner with his father tonight. He told me he would contact me when they were done."

"Have you heard from him?" Rae could hear the edge in Eve's voice.

"No. Have either of you heard from Jules?"

Both women said no and Rae closed her eyes. She could feel the pounding in her head intensifying. Trying not to overreact, she took several deep breaths to stabilize her emotions, but she couldn't get the photos out of her head.

"I will try to call him. I'll talk to you later?"

"Yeah."

"Sure."

"Bye."

Rae found Flint's phone number in her recent phone calls and clicked it. The phone rang and rang until it went to his voice mail. Rae sucked her teeth and threw her phone down on the counter. Shaking her head at herself, she picked up her phone and checked to make sure it was still in working order. She texted Eve and Liv what had happened.

Rae: *No answer.*

Liv: *Should we text Jules?*

Eve: *I think we should. She seems to be the potential link to all of this.*

Rae: *I agree.*

There was silence for a bit before Rae heard her text ringtone.

Liv: *Hey Jules. Where are you?*

Time seemed to slow down as Rae waited for Jules to respond. Her heart jumped when she heard her phone go off once more. That excitement and nervousness were short-lived when she realized it was a spam message.

Rae wasn't sure how long she stared at her wall in silence. The blank screen of her TV showed nothing but her sad reflection looking back at her. Being alone with just her thoughts was dangerous.

A knock on the door brought her back to reality. Her phone flashed 9:34 p.m. and no new notifications. The radio silence from Jules and Flint was deafening.

She checked through the peephole before opening the door.

"I thought you guys weren't coming over?"

"You thought we wouldn't come over when you were going through a mini-crisis? Get real," Liv said as she scooted past Rae and let herself into her apartment. Eve hugged her before closing the door behind her. The trio headed to Rae's couch and plopped down.

"So when can we kick his ass?"

Rae chuckled and shook her head at Liv's comment. "I want an explanation. More than that, Jules not responding is driving me nuts."

Rae put her head in her hands and felt Eve throw her arm around her shoulders as she consoled her.

"Hello? Jules?"

Rae's and Eve's heads shot up as they looked at Liv. She did always take life by the horns, so the duo wasn't shocked that she had just called her.

"Hey! Are you busy? Did you just get out of the fundraiser? You need to come over to Rae's apartment."

Rae tuned out the rest of the conversation because her thoughts consumed her. She reached up to wipe the tears she knew had fallen but found none. At least they had stopped for now.

"Okay, see you soon." And with that, Liv hung up the phone, but then was silent.

"So?" Eve asked. Liv didn't respond right away. Rae raised an eyebrow as she waited for Liv to speak.

"Jules didn't respond to our text because she didn't get it until just now. Apparently, there was poor service in the building they were in, but she's headed over here. And she was the one who brought up Flint."

Rae's blood turned to ice. "Did she tell you anything?"

"Not really, but she told me to grab some wine because we wouldn't believe this."

Jules soon arrived at Rae's apartment and began to share what she had seen at the event.

FLINT WALKED into the room and immediately found his parents. A bunch of people surrounded them, probably shooting the shit. If you could say anything about his father, he was, without a doubt, a master networker and always knew someone who knew something about someone else. And he definitely used that to his advantage.

Somewhat ignoring his parents on the other side of the room, he mingled with his coworkers and some other guests. He didn't know how much time had passed before he heard someone call his name. He swung around and saw his mom smiling at him. Although she didn't work in the realm of politics, it was assumed that she would attend these events with her husband.

"Sweetie, can I speak to you for a second?"

Flint nodded and followed his mother to a quiet corner on the other side of the ballroom.

"Is everything all right?"

"Yes, dear. Why would you think it isn't?"

"Because you asked me to follow you over here."

"That doesn't mean that anything is wrong."

Flint was losing his patience with his mother. "Please stop evading my question. What is going on?"

She sighed before saying, "I need you to break up with Rae."

He did a double-take before replying, "Excuse me?!"

"Keep your voice down, dear."

Flint raked a hand through his hair before saying, "I'm not breaking up with Rae."

"You will if you want a decent shot at that congressional seat."

"Excuse me?" Flint knew he sounded like a broken record, but couldn't find any other words to say.

"I believe that you heard what I said."

"Doesn't make it any less ludicrous. What do I being with Rae have anything to do with me running for a congressional seat that is technically not even up for grabs yet?"

"Well, that's the thing. You need to be dating Cassandra Hopkins to seal the deal."

His mother had to have lost her mind. "You are telling me Cassandra, and I need to date to ensure that I end up with an advantage in the primary?" He figured repeating his mother would show her that what she said was crazy.

"Ensure is a strong word, but certain things might work out in your favor if you do."

"What things?"

"I'm not at liberty to discuss, but I will say some contribution to a campaign might be at stake."

It took every ounce of control in his body not to swear. "Mom, this is unreasonable," he whispered.

"It's the only way. So it's either Rae or your political future. And I suggest you make your decision quickly." And with that, she gave him a soft pat on the shoulder and walked away.

Flint didn't move for several seconds. He took a deep breath and headed toward the men's bathroom, which he had spotted when he had followed his mom, figuring that would buy him a few more minutes before he had to face anyone else.

But what he hadn't known was that someone else, lurking in the shadows, had heard his conversation with his mother. And she knew just what she would do with this information.

"THAT'S WHAT I HEARD." The silence after Jules's statement was palpable.

"And here I thought I was the one who was the next Nancy Drew. Jules, you beat me to it!" Liv exclaimed. Her comment broke some tension in the room.

"So, how did the picture come about?"

Jules shrugged. "So I guess I should point out I'm not sure what happened after Flint's conversation with his mother. Flint and I talked for a few moments, but I couldn't ask him about what I heard. While we were talking to another group of people, one photographer who was walking around at the time asked us to get a group picture. We were standing together, and I saw something flash out of the corner of my eye, but it wasn't from the photographer's camera. So I turned and saw that Cassandra had plopped herself between Flint and me. I didn't even know she would be at the event, but there she was in all of her glory. She was up in his personal space and he didn't seem to try to get away from her."

"Have you heard from him at all?"

Rae shook her head at Jules's question. Not even a text message to check-in and make sure everything was all right with her day or anything?

"We can spend the night if you want us to. That way, you won't be alone."

Rae thought about it for a second before nodding. "Thanks, you guys."

"Whew, I'm glad you agreed because Eve and I already packed a bag just in case. Our bags are in the car." Liv left the room as she went to grab their bags.

Rae laughed before turning to Jules and saying, "I can probably give you something to wear for tonight and to wear home. We are about the same size."

Jules smiled at her friend and patted her on the hand. "Sounds like a plan. Oh, Rae?"

Rae turned her attention back to Jules.

"Do you want me to call Flint?"

Rae didn't respond right away. She didn't know what the right answer to this situation was, but she went with her gut. "No, don't call him. I have already reached out to him, and if he wants to talk to me, he knows how."

Eve reached over and gave Rae a one-armed hug. "It will be okay. You got through this before, and you'll get through it again. Plus, at the very least, we are going on vacation in a few days."

With everything that had been going on, Rae had

completely forgotten about the vacation. At least she had that to look forward to.

Liv soon came back into the apartment, carrying two duffel bags that she placed in the living room. At Rae's direction, Eve found a king-size blow-up mattress and brought it into the living room. Rae found an extra pair of sheets, blankets, and snatched some pillows off her bed to make the girls feel more comfortable in her living room. Once they were all set up, Liv reached into her bag and pulled out three more bottles of wine.

Eve looked at her with disbelief. "When did you have time to pick those up?"

"I was in the supermarket when I sent the first text message. I had originally bought these for me, myself, and I, but I figured this situation was dire."

"Thanks, Liv," Rae said as she looked at Liv. She then turned to Jules, who was doing everything in her power to hold back her laughter.

"Don't worry about it. I always come prepared."

"And I think I can speak for all of us and say that we're all grateful for that."

23

A loud knocking stirred Rae from her sleep. The grogginess she was experiencing had won control over her body, so she turned over and further buried herself in the covers. When the noise continued, she surveyed the room and realized that she was in her bedroom. It must have been early morning based on the sun's positioning outside her window. She didn't know how she ended up in her bed, but she was proud to have made it there after the ruckus they had caused the night before. The quiet was short-lived when she heard what she thought was pounding on her door. The noise was enough to get her adrenaline running and her moving out of bed.

Her heart was racing as she ran to her closet to get a hoodie to put over the tank top and shorts that she had fallen asleep in. When had she changed into these shorts? She didn't have a clue. Was the building on fire? She couldn't smell any smoke, but that didn't mean that it wasn't. On that thought, should she be wasting her time putting a sweatshirt on?

Before she could open her door, she heard arguing coming from her living room.

"What are you doing here?!"

She was sure all of her neighbors in a fifty-mile radius more than likely heard Liv's question. Rae scrambled to her bedroom door to listen to what was going on in her apartment.

"I came to see Rae." The rich timbre she had fallen in love with immediately responded to the question. Rae poked her head out into the hallway to see the commotion.

"She's sleeping like most people would be at seven-thirty in the morning on a Saturday. So not only did you wake us up, but you probably woke up half the block with your knocking. By the way, you look like shit." Liv's arms were folded and her glare was firmly in place. Rae knew that she didn't want to be in Flint's shoes right now.

"Well, I'm glad I look the way I feel."

So Flint had come to her apartment this morning to talk to her, she assumed. The rest of last night started flowing back into her memory. He could have waited until at least 10:00 a.m. Although she'd had fun, she was feeling it this morning, especially with this 7:30 a.m. wake-up call.

Rae bounded back to her bed and picked up her phone she'd thrown to the side as she was getting up to answer her front door.

She opened her text messages and scrolled through to see if Flint had texted her back after her messages to him last night, but there was nothing. So the plan was to ambush her at home? She tucked her phone into the pocket of her hoodie before heading into the living room to face the music.

"What's all this noise about?" Rae asked as soon as she

entered the hallway. Liv was standing at the door glaring at Flint, while Eve and Jules were sitting on the couch, looking like they were deciding between staying seated and saving Flint's life if Liv launched at him, and it looked like she might launch herself at him.

"Rae," Flint said, her name softly falling off his lips. Liv wasn't lying about him looking like shit. His green T-shirt and blue jeans were crinkled. His hair was going every which way as if he had spent most of the night pulling at it. The bags under his bloodshot eyes were new and made him look as if he hadn't slept all night. The morning scruff that made her swoon today made him look more unkempt. And the twinkle in his eyes she loved to see was gone.

"What are you doing here?"

"I wanted to talk to you about last night. I was hoping we could talk alone."

"Yeah, no."

"What?" The look of puzzlement on Flint's face almost made her laugh.

"What are you confused about? I don't want to talk to you alone, so you can say whatever you want right here."

Flint took his time, looking at the women in the room, who were shooting daggers at him. When his eyes landed on her, all he could do was stare.

"Ahem." Rae cleared her throat and waited for him to continue.

Flint walked over to where Rae was standing near her bedroom door.

"Rae, I'm so sorry for not responding to your message right away. I had seen it, but I kept getting distracted."

"Why didn't you send me a text message after the party?"

"Because I couldn't find my phone. Hell, I still don't know where it is."

"I guess you left it at the venue."

"I don't think I did. I'm not entirely sure," Flint said as he checked his pockets once again. His eyes were pleading with Rae to forgive him, but she was having none of it.

"Looks like you need to get it replaced, then. Why are you here, Flint?" The fact that she wasn't a blubbering mess right now made her proud.

"Rae, I'm sorry all of this went down. I lo—"

"What was going on with you and Cassandra? Are you breaking up with me for her?" The words didn't sound logical as they flew out of her mouth, but she was pissed and didn't care.

Flint whipped his head back as if someone slapped him. "No, not in this lifetime or the next if I can help it. Why?"

Rae turned to Liv and asked, "Could you pull up the photo from last night?"

Liv produced the photo, handed her phone to Rae, and Rae shoved it in Flint's face.

"So, can you explain this?" Rae gestured to the phone in her hand.

Flint stared at the photo but said nothing.

Rae nodded her head and handed the phone back to Liv.

"Rae, can I please talk to you alone?"

Her mind told her this was something she didn't have to do, but her heart was asking her to give him a chance. With a sigh, she beckoned him to come into her room. He followed her and closed the door gently behind them.

Rae pulled her phone out of her hoodie pocket and set a timer. "You have three minutes."

Flint said nothing for a few seconds. He just stared at her until she had had enough.

Clearing her throat, she said, "Looks like your time is now down to two minutes and forty-five seconds."

Flint raked a hand through his hair as his eyes darted around the room. And that's how she figured he had gotten the hairstyle mentioned above that he was sporting this morning.

"Last night got out of hand."

When Rae did nothing but fold her arms, he sighed and continued, "I'm not even sure where to begin."

"The beginning would be nice."

"That does probably make the most sense. So as you very well know, I attended a fundraising event last night. My parents were there along with Jules."

Rae nodded her head and gestured for him to continue.

"So, my mom came up to me during the event and essentially said I need to break up with you if I want any shot at a political future."

Rae's arms remained crossed as she listened as Flint explained his side of the story.

"Some people who are very involved in Virginia politics told my parents that it would look better if I were dating Cassandra, given that her family is also heavily involved in Virginia politics as well. It would help guarantee money for my campaign."

Even hearing the words for a second time caused Rae's heart to career out of control. She chose her next words carefully. "I don't understand. The whole point of your fundraising was so you wouldn't have to depend on one particular group of people to donate a huge amount of money to your campaign. That's the hypothetical vision you laid out when you talked about running a couple of weeks ago."

"I know, and I thought about taking their deal last night."

"Is that what led to the photos of you and Cassandra that were floating around social media last night?"

All Flint did was nod. Rae checked her phone before saying, "Good job. You came in at under three minutes. Now leave." The coldness in her voice reflected the iciness she felt for him in her heart.

"Please. I was selfish and stupid. And you are right. We agreed to certain parameters when we talked about this before. I'm sorry. It was a lapse in judgment."

"That is an understatement. Please leave." Rae mentally scolded herself when she said, please. It was her apartment, and right now, she didn't want to be polite.

Flint nodded his head before opening her bedroom door. He glanced back at her before closing the door and exiting her life once again. At that realization, she sat down on her bed and cried.

"You know you guys have lives as well? You don't have to babysit me. Go home and do the things you have to do."

Rae and her girlfriends had hung around her house most of the morning after Flint had left. They had done everything they could to help Rae deal with the initial shock of the breakup and the rollercoaster of emotions she was on.

"If that's what you want us to do. You know we want to be

here for you," Eve said from her seat on the other end of the couch.

"Yes, but not to the detriment of yourselves. I'm sure y'all have last-minute to-dos and errands to run before our vacation."

Liv nodded her head as Jules stood up from her spot on the floor. Each friend helped Rae clean the mess they made in the kitchen and the living room before saying their good-byes and heading for the front door.

"Rae, if you need anything, reach out, okay?" Eve said as Rae was getting ready to close the door.

"I know, and thank you so much." The two shared one last hug before Rae closed and locked the door behind them. "Might as well get some things done around the house."

She walked over to her phone, turned on some music, and got to work. She carried her phone from room to room as she threw some food into her Crock-Pot so she wouldn't have to worry about cooking dinner or ordering takeout. Rae then walked into her bedroom and pulled out the laundry she wanted to do, along with all the bedding she now had to wash. Thankful that she had a washer and dryer in her unit, she got to work on that. As Rae was tidying up her bedroom, she heard her phone ring. Stealing a glance away from her task, she checked the caller ID and noticed that it was an unknown number. Not having time for those shenanigans, she sent it to voice mail before going back to the task at hand.

About a minute later, her phone pinged, and the second intrusion caused her to roll her eyes. She swore if this were the same person who had just called her she would—

"What the hell?"

Unknown Number: *You did the right thing.*

What creep would text those words? Rae looked closer at the number and realized something about it. The area code triggered a memory. She scanned her blocked numbers and saw there was only one other number she had blocked with that area code. It was the number that sent her messages about leaving Flint alone years ago.

24

Rae didn't know what to do with this information. She couldn't exactly go to Flint with it since they were currently broken up. Deciding that it wasn't worth burdening her friends, Rae blocked that number as well and went back to the chores she needed to do around the house. When she was done, she decided that a shower and a relaxing evening were in order. Rae wiped away what she assumed was tears from her eyes. It could have also been water from the showerhead as she tried to relax after a long day at work.

The days dawdled along as Rae eagerly anticipated the girls' trip to Bermuda. It didn't help matters that all Rae could think about was Flint. He had texted her a couple of times, but Rae ignored the messages because she wasn't ready to deal with him.

Rae found herself awake bright and early. This was the first time in a while she had felt somewhat normal since the incident with Flint. She stretched before getting out of bed and grabbing the clothes she laid out for herself on her dresser the night before. After changing into her clothes, she headed to her bathroom to finish doing a couple of things in there. Brushing her teeth was first on the list before washing her face. When she was done, she caught herself staring in her bathroom mirror. She should try to get the last-minute items into her carry-on, but here she was.

Her phone's ringtone brought her out of her thoughts. She checked her phone and saw that it was just her alarm and grabbed her toiletries. Placing them in her carry-on was another thing off of her mental to-do list. When Rae thought she had done all the tasks she needed to do that morning, she did one more run-through of her apartment before calling a taxi to head to DCA for her flight in three hours.

Rae made it to the airport in record time, and Jules was the first one to greet her. She was sure Eve and Liv only grunted at her arrival. Jules had always been an early bird like her, whereas both Eve and Liv could sleep until noon if given a chance.

"This morning is going that well for the two of you, huh?"

Eve snorted while Liv gave her answer with a one-finger salute. Rae smirked and sat down in the seat next to Jules.

"Sorry, I'm a little late."

Jules waved her off and shook her head. "Oh, wait, this is for you." Jules bent down, grabbed a cup, and handed it to Rae.

"And this is why we're friends. Thanks." She took a sip from the coffee that Jules had bought while Rae was in the security line. She sighed as the liquid flowed through her body, providing an extra boost of energy.

"I don't understand how you can drink coffee black. And don't worry about paying me back."

Rae nodded and said, "It's a talent."

Jules shook her head before turning her attention back to her phone.

"I don't understand how you two can carry on a conversation this early in the morning. I can't wait to get on the plane and pass out." Part of Eve's comment came out jumbled, but Rae could put two and two together. Eve raised the hood of her sweatshirt over her head, placed her headphones in her ears, and sunk lower in her chair. Rae was sure Liv had fallen asleep on the two chairs to the left of Eve.

"How are you doing?" Jules's question grabbed Rae's attention as she took another sip of coffee.

"In general, or about Flint?"

"Both?"

"I'm all right. Weepier than usual, but that could be hormones too."

"Have you heard from him?"

Rae didn't move. It made sense, to tell the truth, so she reached into her bag and pulled out her phone. She found her text messages and handed the phone to Jules.

Flint: I'm so sorry for everything that I've done and everything that has happened. I shouldn't have entertained the idea of pretending to be in a relationship with Cassandra when it's you I want to be with. If you're ever ready to talk, I'm here.

And a few days later he sent this:

Flint: Hey Rae. I just wanted to reach out and make sure you were okay.

She hadn't responded to either message.

"At least he knows he was wrong. Some people can't even admit that and knowing that is half the battle."

Rae nodded along with her. "Has he said anything to you?"

Jules shook her head and said, "No, but I'll let you know if he does."

"Okay," said Rae as she turned her attention to the television that displayed their flight information as she waited to board.

RAE STEPPED off the plane and breathed a sigh of relief. They had just arrived in Bermuda, and she immediately felt the stress roll off her shoulders. She tried to push Flint to the back of her mind so she could focus on what she wanted. For now and in the future.

Eve put an arm around Rae's shoulders as they walked toward the baggage claim. "Are you feeling okay? Your face is saying one thing, but that's unacceptable since we're in Bermuda, and you should be happy."

"I'm fine." Rae let the lie slide right off her lips. "I'm having a hard time processing everything is all. It annoys me he didn't believe me about his mother. I get it because it's his mother, but the signs were all there. She doesn't even know me."

"She doesn't care about knowing you. She wanted to do whatever she could to help Flint get elected to Congress, and that included trying to meddle with his dating life. Which is crazy."

"It also hurt me that Flint somewhat went along with it. I understand that she's his mother, but he knew what she was doing was wrong and would hurt me. Yet here we are."

"True. But at least you're taking time out for yourself," Jules said as she and Liv strolled up behind Rae and Eve. She grabbed Rae's arm and pulled them toward the carousel, where they were supposed to pick up their luggage. The wait to get their bags took a little longer than they expected, but they weren't worse for wear. They walked toward the exit and looked for a driver holding a sign with Liv's name on it since she was the one who ended up booking the trip.

"I can't believe we're here!" Liv exclaimed while she settled into the resort shuttle. She had napped on the plane to Bermuda and that sleep had given her a boost of energy. Or maybe she'd had some spiked orange juice, which wouldn't be out of character.

Rae pulled Jules aside. "She didn't have too much on the plane, right? Is she going to pass out as soon as we reach the resort?"

Jules smirked before replying, "She may have had one mimosa. I think she's just acting like Liv."

Rae breathed a sigh of relief. She knew Liv could handle herself, but she didn't want the first memory of Bermuda being Liv passed out on the living room floor of their beautiful suite. Well, at least based on the pictures it appeared to be beautiful.

The ride to the resort was uneventful, but once they reached the entrance, all thoughts that had consumed the girls' minds went out the window.

"This is stunning," Liv said as the group looked around the grounds from the shuttle. The palm trees were lightly blowing in the wind as they drove down the road to what Rae assumed was their suite. The resort had motel style buildings that were two floors high. But the driver kept going. The women shared a look between them as he kept driving down the windy road. When he slowed down, everyone else's mouths were wide open.

"Welcome to paradise," he said, looking at the women in the rearview mirror.

And paradise it was.

AFTER CHECKING IN, the women hopped back on the shuttle to go to their lodging. The driver stopped the vehicle and started unloading the luggage. The women offered to help him, and when he opened the door to their suite, their mouths were wide open. The bungalow where they were staying was beautiful. The driver handed Rae her items first, and she waited for her friends to grab their things before she headed to the room. When the driver opened the door, the women were frozen by the scene in front of them.

"Um, Liv, are you sure this is what you booked us?"

Liv didn't answer for a few seconds before letting out a high-pitched squeal. "Yes! I didn't think it would look this beautiful, though!"

The women made their way into the suite, too stunned to do anything besides look around. When they stepped across the threshold, their living room, which had couches facing the balcony overlooking the beach and the ocean, greeted them. Connected to the living room was the dining room with colorful flowers on the table and a nice-sized kitchen that had upgraded appliances.

"Is there anything else I can get you?"

"No, sir. Thanks so much." Jules was the only one who could find the words to say.

"Welcome to Bermuda," their driver said before he left their suite.

"We should check out the bedrooms, huh? Let's meet at the resort lounge fifteen minutes before our lunch reservation. Just in case anyone wants to enjoy a beverage." Eve asked as she led the way to the back where they assumed the bedrooms were. When Rae opened the door of the room she had chosen, she was blown away.

"Someone's speaking my language," Rae mumbled as she continued to take in the room. Her bed looked to be a king and was made up of soft sheets and a plethora of pillows she was used to on her bed.

She walked down the hall and came across one of the two bathrooms and noticed it had a tub and shower. Rae knew she had to get in the tub at least once during her stay at the resort. Walking back into her room, she began unpacking her stuff and settling in. The fact that Rae was here on this island right now was blowing her mind. Its beauty shocked her, and she knew that she wanted to just stare out at the ocean while relaxing by herself. Rae made a mental note to get up earlier in the morning to watch the sunrise over the ocean.

She continued unpacking her things and placing them where she could quickly grab them without thinking too much about it. She unpacked some of the clothes she thought might easily wrinkle because she wanted to avoid having to iron for as long as possible. Although she knew she was supposed to meet up with the girls in a little while, all she wanted to do was go to bed. And that made her feel guilty because they were on vacation.

Rae freshened up and changed into a peach sundress. She put on a bit of perfume and grabbed her phone and her purse before she headed out to meet her friends at the main lodge. Her sandals slapped against the pavement as she quickly walked to her destination. The heat wasn't as bad as it could get in DC because of the humidity is high, which made Rae happy. A man and woman were walking out of the lodge and held the doors open as she walked through them. Taking the time to enjoy the air conditioning, Rae looked around until she spotted Liv sitting alone in the resort lobby. Liv was doing something on her phone, choosing to ignore the world around her.

"Here, you are on vacation, and you're planning on staying on your phone the entire time?" Rae said as Liv smirked and glanced her way. She typed a couple of more things before she sat up and looked up from her phone.

"I was just catching up on some work emails before I completely went dark."

Rae nodded and plopped into a seat next to Liv. "That makes sense. I should probably do the same," Rae said as she took out her phone. She saw that she had a few emails, but none of them were pressing. Double-checking that she turned her vacation email responder on, she put her phone in her purse as she turned to Liv.

"Is everything okay with you?"

"Yeah, why?"

"Because you haven't glanced up from your phone at all."

Liv sighed and placed her phone down. She rubbed her face and blinked several times before she looked at Rae. "Sorry about that. Things have just been crazy recently."

"Are you sure it's just about work?"

"Yeah. Everything is fine. Don't worry about it."

Rae knew better than to push Liv, even though she suspected that something else was up. When Liv was ready to tell her what was up, she would.

"Did you hear anything from Eve or Jules? They'll make us late for our reservation."

"Nope. Did they text you? And don't worry about the reservation."

Rae pulled out her phone and saw nothing from her other two friends. She had a text notification from Flint. She debated reading the message but thought better of it. She was on vacation and should try to keep as much of the drama that she left in DC there.

Before she could second-guess her decision, Jules and Eve hurried up to them. The two were out of breath.

"What happened to you guys?" Rae asked.

"We were just running late and bumped into each other on the way out. I'm sorry I kept you both waiting." Jules reached over to get a tissue off the end table closest to Liv. She handed a tissue to Eve, and they both wiped the sweat that had formed after their workout.

"Shit. Did we mess up the reservation? I know you said 1:15." Eve held out her hand for Jules's tissue, and once Jules handed it over, Eve walked to the small garbage can near the front desk and threw both of them out.

"I told you guys 1:15, but our reservation is at 1:30. I added a little buffer just in case someone lost track of time. Figured whoever came at 1:15 would have no problem hanging out at the bar for a little while." Rae couldn't find a flaw in Liv's logic and was thankful that she came up with the idea.

"Good idea. Seeing as how it's 1:27, should we head to the hostess desk?"

Everyone agreed, and the four friends walked up to the hostess and were seated within a couple of minutes. The group looked over the menu and noticed that they had an enormous amount of options between going up to a buffet and ordering one of ten entrée options on the menu. There were also plenty of drinks, alcoholic, and nonalcoholic that they could choose from. All the food and nonalcoholic beverages were included in their package.

"Well, since it's a vacation and I am no longer dieting to fit into a bathing suit, I'm digging in," announced Liv. Rae was in the middle of skimming the menu when she noticed that her phone screen briefly lit up. Having decided what she wanted to eat and drink, she figured it would be all right to check it while the girls were still choosing and waiting for their server to arrive. It was another message from Flint.

Rae sighed before putting her phone facedown on the table. Thankfully, no one noticed her motions as they were perusing the menu.

The server came back up to the table and took everyone's food and drink order, and filled their water glasses before he left.

"I think we should make a toast when our drinks arrive," Rae said.

"Cheers to what?" Jules asked, turning her full attention to Rae.

"Cheers to a girls' vacation and leaving behind the drama setting DC on fire at the moment. Well, at least in my small neck of the woods."

"I totally understand that," Eve said as she took a sip of her water.

To the surprise of the table, the waiter returned with their drinks quickly, and Liv cleared her throat.

"To us. Because loving and having faith in ourselves and each other will help us get through the rough times and celebrate the good."

"Cheers!"

25

────────

Rae was on cloud nine as she and her girlfriends walked back to their suite. They had spent the rest of their day exploring different parts of the resort. Lunch and dinner had been fantastic, and the drinks were everything they hoped they would be and more. The smiles on their faces couldn't be tamed and their giggles were infectious. They spent most of the day exploring their resort. She couldn't remember the last time they had all had this much fun, or she felt so free. The quartet said good-night, and Rae closed the door of her bedroom. Silence greeted her, and that was when her thoughts came out to play.

Her phone had been teasing her all night. Although she tried to act like she didn't care, the thought of Flint sending her texts had her stomach in knots for most of the night. The texts from Flint probably led to her being even more enthusiastic about the drinks that kept coming to their table at lunch and dinner.

Figuring that it was only a matter of time before exhaustion would take over, she started getting ready for bed. When she finished her nighttime routine and was lying in bed, her eyes kept darting back over to her phone, which was charging on the end table. Shaking her head at herself, she grabbed the phone and checked her text messages to see who had reached out to her besides Flint.

Seeing a message from her parents, she replied to them before the haunting thoughts returned. Should she or shouldn't she check to see what Flint had said to her?

"Screw it," mumbled Rae.

Flint: Did you make it to Bermuda okay?

Flint: I again just wanted to tell you how sorry I truly am.

Rae knew she shouldn't have checked the messages because she had been drinking; she knew it would make her feel some kind of way.

How did he remember that she was going to Bermuda? She hadn't mentioned it recently, so she went to find the only person who probably would have said it to him.

"Jules?" Rae asked as she walked into the living room of their suite. She found Eve in the kitchen, grabbing a snack and Liv lounging on the couch in front of the TV. But no Jules.

"Where did Jules go?"

"Bathroom. I assume she'll be out in a minute unless she got swallowed by the toilet monster."

"Ha. Ha. Ha. You're hilarious," Jules said as she walked into the living room. "What's up?" she asked, turning her attention to Rae.

"Did Flint reach out to you?"

Jules frowned before saying, "I don't think so, but I've been intentionally avoiding my phone all day so he might have. Let me go get it." She grabbed her bag and brought it over toward Rae as she was trying to find her phone.

"Let's move this to the couch," Eve said as she walked around the two women and into the living room. Rae and Jules followed, and by the times Jules sat down, she had pulled her phone out from the jungle that was her purse and was scanning through it to see if there was anything from Flint.

"Looks like he sent me something." She showed her phone to Rae, who then shared it with the rest of the group.

Flint: Hey, did you, Rae, Eve, and Liv go to Bermuda?

Flint: I stopped by Rae's hoping to talk to her, and she didn't answer the door. I texted her, but have heard nothing, so I figured the next best option was you since I don't have any contact information for her parents.

Flint: Sorry, didn't mean to send all of those messages, but I just wanted to know that y'all were okay.

"That was sweet of him, I guess," Liv said. Rae knew Liv was still regretting not snapping at him more when he was standing at Rae's door several days ago.

"I guess I could at least tell him I'm fine," Rae said out loud, and Eve nodded along with her. "Or I could just ask you to confirm I'm fine."

"Honestly, I'd do it if you wanted me to, but I also would kind of like to stay out of this."

"Don't blame you there, girl," Eve said as she leaned over to give Jules a high five.

"I know you're right. I'll text Flint back," Rae said as she eyed her phone in her hand. She unlocked the phone and started typing.

Rae: We are in Bermuda and everything is fine. Thanks for checking.

And with that, she clicked her phone off and placed it facedown on the coffee table.

"Do y'all want to do anything tonight? Or should we just head to bed and get up early tomorrow?"

Liv looked at her and huffed. "How about we stay in and sleep late too? There is nothing wrong with that. You and Jules are freaks of nature."

Jules shook her head as Rae nudged Liv with her elbow.

"If that's what we want to do, that's fine. Jules, you want to head to the gym early tomorrow then while these two catch their z's?"

"That sounds like a plan."

"Okay, well, I'll see y'all tomorrow." After bidding everyone farewell, Rae walked back into her room and shut the door.

"Do you have any idea what we're doing for the rest of the day?" Rae asked while taking a glimpse at Jules. They made their workout session the next morning while Liv and Eve caught up on their sleep.

"Nope. Liv has shared nothing else with me, but I wouldn't be surprised if it didn't include something like lying on the beach for most of the day."

"I, for one, wouldn't be mad at that." Rae turned up the speed on her treadmill and began jogging.

"Same. Did you hear anything else from Flint?"

"Kind of. He said thanks for letting him know and that

was it." The words came out in a hurry because Rae was trying to concentrate on her workout.

"Huh. That's a bit of a change from what he was doing before."

Rae nodded before replying, "I was thinking the same thing." She turned down the speed on the treadmill before setting it to a pace that she could keep up with by speed walking. "Okay, I didn't expect that to knock the wind out of me at that speed."

"You were also trying to talk during it."

"True. Rookie mistake." Rae slowed her pace down even more and took that time to catch her breath. "Do you want to do some weights before we head back?"

Jules nodded as she stopped the machine. She hopped off her treadmill, while Rae slowed hers down to a stop. Jules walked back over to Rae with a rag and cleaning solution, and the two took the time to wipe down their treadmills before they headed over to the weight machines.

Although they were spending one morning of their vacation working out, Rae couldn't complain. The gym at the resort was empty beside them, and they got to spend the morning looking at the ocean as they got their workout in for the day. The women did a thirty-minute weight-training workout that Jules found online before grabbing their things and heading back to their suite.

When they arrived, Liv's and Eve's bedroom doors were still closed, so they figured that now would be the best time to shower so that the bathrooms would be free for Eve and Liv. By the time they finished their showers, Liv and Eve were up and ready to go.

"Did you guys just want to hang out at the beach today and maybe head to the crystal caves tomorrow?"

Jules gave Rae a smirk after Liv finished her question. The women agreed that this was a great plan, and Rae headed to her room to put on her bathing suit. The dark green bikini made her golden-brown skin glisten even more.

She gave herself a once-over in the mirror. "This bathing suit was a good purchase," she said to herself.

After thinking about it for a few moments, she put her hair in a braided ponytail. Putting her black coverup on, she debated wearing jewelry. Deciding against it because she would go into the water, Rae grabbed the things she wanted to take with her to the beach and placed them in a tote she brought from home.

She walked out of her room and met the other women in their living room.

"Is everyone ready to head out?" A chorus of yeses rang out, and the girls grabbed their belongings and walked down to the beach.

"So Jules, were you trying to block out the entire sun with that hat of yours? I'm sure if we all stood in front of you, we would think it was a cloudy day."

Rae shook her head at Liv as she laughed at her own joke.

"I'll have you know that I burn easily, so I bought the biggest hat I could find. Don't think you won't burn, too, just because your skin tans better than mine."

"True, but that's why I bought a baseball cap and sunscreen. It will—"

Liv stopped midsentence once she reached their destination.

"So this is where the parties happen," Liv said as she

examined their location. Rae spun around in a circle as she tried to take in the scenery. To her left was a decent-size pool with a swim-up bar. It had pool chairs, umbrellas, and tables. She thought she spotted menus, which made her assume that there would be servers that would take their orders right at their seats versus having to go up to the bar. When Rae looked to the right, down a set of stairs was a beach with beach chairs and umbrellas right off the ocean.

"Where do we want to go first?" Eve asked.

"Anywhere that allows me to sit under an umbrella because I don't want to fry." Jules fanned herself and adjusted her big sun hat. Rae took that moment to place her sunglasses on her face.

"Why don't we head to the beach, so we can lounge or play in the ocean if we want?" Eve gestured to the stairs.

"You're the voice of reason. Let's go." Rae smirked at Liv's retort before the girls walked toward the stairs.

The girls found four beach chairs near each other and claimed them by leaving the beach things they brought with them on the seats. Luckily, the four chairs had two umbrellas already set up, so they didn't have to worry about dragging one down from another set of chairs.

"How about the two of us go get drinks, while you two get towels for the group?" Rae said as she grabbed her phone. She saw that she had a notification, but ignored it until they were all settled at the beach.

"Sounds good. How about me and Jules go get drinks, and you and Eve go get the towels?" Liv said as she stood up next to the chair she selected. The group agreed and decided that they all wanted different flavored margaritas before they headed off in their separate directions.

Rae and Eve walked silently along the beach on the way to get some towels. Rae checked her phone and noticed another text notification. She ignored it while Eve spoke.

"How's everything going?" Eve asked as she broke the silence floating between them.

"I'm fine." Rae paused before correcting her statement. "It sucks that my automatic response is to say I'm fine when I'm not. I'm trying to change that habit, but it seems to be a hard one to break. I'm doing better than I expected, but I still feel heartbroken, still have a million questions that I would like to ask."

"No one is stopping you from asking those questions. And I believe that habit is something we all do, and it will take time to break."

"I know, but I am supposed to be moving on and getting over all this."

"Sometimes, to take a step forward, we need to take a step back. Examine what happened, so we don't make the same mistakes again."

"But I feel like I am making a mistake by thinking about this so much." Rae sighed as she tried to rein in her emotions.

"That's okay. The breakup is still fresh, and you're allowed to think about it fifty million times. Plus, you overthink anyway, so this isn't shocking." Rae nudged Eve in the stomach with her elbow before shaking her head. "But seriously, I get it."

"I'm just...confused. If Flint wanted to be with Cassandra, he could just be with her. I would let him go if it meant that he was happy even if it was with someone else."

"Maybe he doesn't want to be with Cassandra."

Rae lifted her sunglasses and glanced over at Eve to see if she was serious.

"Do you know something that I don't know?"

"Nope. I just find it very odd how serious you two were, then for him to turn around and act as though Cassandra posing up against him was like a stab to the back. I mean, he wanted your opinion on how you felt about him running for political office. To go from that to the whole Cassandra incident seems weird. But stranger things have happened.

"Having that in mind, do you think it's possible that the camera snapped what it wanted you to see and that you should talk to Flint? This time when you aren't as upset? It doesn't mean that you need to forgive him or jump back into a relationship with him. The conversation might just be you need to seek more information to make an informed decision."

By the time Rae and Eve reached the towels, Rae hadn't said a word. Eve's advice was helpful, and she was trying to process everything to figure out her steps forward. She grabbed two towels and handed two towels to Eve before they set back on their journey toward the beach chairs.

"You know I thought we would be together and make it work this time. We are older and wiser and know more about what we can do to make this relationship work. Or so I thought."

"There is still time to heal the rift between you two if that's what you want to do."

"That's the thing, I'm not sure what I want to do." Rae paused, gently pulling on her braided ponytail that had made its way over her shoulder. She then threw it back over her shoulder, where it belonged. She was happy she chose that hairstyle because it kept all of her hair in one place and allowed her to adjust her hair with ease. By the end of the day, chances were that her hair would be a frizzy mess anyway, but for now, it looked good. "Actually, that's a lie. I love him, but this is a lot. Do you think reaching out to him would provide the answers I'm looking for?" Rae asked that question softly as if it scared her to find out what Eve thought.

"It could. But it could also open up a can of worms I don't think you want to touch right now, but that doesn't mean you shouldn't try to talk to him. After all, you are adults. What's the worst that could happen?"

I get my heart broken all over again.

A LITTLE WHILE LATER, JULES' voice brought Rae out of her own thoughts. "Are you liking that book?"

She put the book she had been reading down at her side. She took her bookmark and put it between the pages before she closed the book.

"Yeah, it's good. You get sucked in pretty easily, and it allows you to sit back and relax. It was a great purchase from one of the convenience stores at the airport."

"Do you want to get into the water? Liv said earlier that it was great," Jules asked as Rae took that opportunity to glimpse at Liv lying on her beach chair while Eve checked her email.

Rae smiled. "The playtime in the water and volleyball knocked the wind out of Liv's sails." Eve and Liv had been playing volleyball with some patrons of the resort and then went into the ocean to cool off. That turned into a lot of splashing of water, and now the result was Liv passed out on her beach chair and Eve scrolling through her phone. "I can go for a quick dip. Did you want to join?"

"No, I just got done reapplying my sunscreen."

"Okay, well, you know where I'll be." Rae stood up and took off her bikini coverup. She then headed down the beach. The sand felt warm on the soles of her feet as she made her way toward the ocean. She glanced down the way and saw other people relaxing and playing in the soft pink sand, and the closer she got to the water, the more the salty sea smell took over her nostrils. Here she was, in paradise, yet all she could do was think about Flint. She thought about what he was doing right this very moment, or how much he would enjoy whatever activity she was doing. He was constantly on her brain, no matter how hard she tried to fight it.

She dunked her head in the water before rising to surface and trying to float on her back. She couldn't tell if she was crying or if it was ocean water that was flowing down her face. Rae took the time to lean back and enjoy the sun that was beaming down on her face. The sun's rays helped her feel alive, which led to a smile forming on her face. She didn't know how to feel or what she wanted to do, but at least for now, everything felt fine.

26

Rae wiped the drop of water that fell on her face. She was unfazed by it because the scene in front of her was mesmerizing. Here she was in the Crystal Caves in Bermuda. The walk down into the caves included over one hundred stairs, which made the journey feel even longer but helped build the anticipation of what they were about to see. The women enjoyed the stories their tour guide told, including jokes about the formations and what they resembled.

The formations were stunning but also maintained a ghostly quality to them. These formations weren't just on the ceiling, but also under the water inside the cave. Rae took a few photos but mostly kept her phone tucked away because she was worried about dropping it into the water.

When the women left the caves, they headed back to the resort for an early dinner. They changed out of the clothes they wore to the caves and into nicer clothes for their meal.

"Should have tried this on before I packed it," Rae told herself as she eyed the dark red maxi dress that was draped over her body. She dug into her suitcase and found some tan wedge shoes that she bought on a whim.

"Sometimes, buying things that you don't need ends up coming in handy." Rae put the shoes on and mentally gave them a thumbs-up. After her time at the beach yesterday, she had to wash her hair and rocked a wavier look. Then Rae headed into the bathroom to put on some makeup before returning to the living room. She was the first one ready to go, so she sat on the couch and played with her phone. She had been ignoring the text notification that she had received yesterday but figured that she couldn't avoid it anymore.

Rae rolled her eyes at the message. This is now the third phone number she would have to block. She knew that she should take it more seriously, but the threats had been... empty besides the dead roses sent to her office. The messages always said something would happen if she didn't stop dating Flint, but nothing ever did.

Rae played with the idea about who this person could be but tabled it when she heard one of her friends walking into the living room. She vowed to do more thinking and research when she got back from dinner.

Rae sat up in the middle of the night after she had been staring at the ceiling of her suite room for what seemed like forever. The group had gotten back from dinner hours ago, but Rae wanted to get some shut-eye before she did more research on who could be sending her these messages. Since she wasn't getting any sleep soon, she needed something else to do. Rae put on a sweatshirt and headed into the living room.

She walked over to her fridge and got some ice cubes to pour into a glass. She then grabbed a bottle of water and poured half of it into the cup before walking over to the couch.

Something was bugging her about the whole picture of Cassandra and Flint floating around on social media thing. Although she had deleted her social media accounts a long time ago, she figured now would be a good time to fire them back up because she wanted to inspect the photo.

She found it and immediately felt a headache forming. She clicked on Flint's name, since they tagged him in the photo, and skimmed his profile, but there wasn't much to it. Or he had made a lot of his information private. She had forgotten that she had deleted him back when they broke up because the memory of their relationship was too much for her to handle. Rae went back to the photo and clicked on Cassandra's profile. She found nothing obnoxious, but she noticed that her family seemed to follow some Pennsylvania sports teams pretty closely.

Something clicked.

"This can't be what I think it is," Rae muttered as she clicked over to Cassandra's contact information. Nothing showed up, but Rae was not deterred. She took a chance and saw what Cassandra's parents were up to because she knew at the very least something connected them to Gladys.

Rae found that Gladys and Marie Hopkins seemed to run in the same social circle as she expected, but there was nothing that popped out about her as she combed over her social media footprint. Although Cassandra had a younger brother, Rae skipped him and went directly to Cassandra's father, Calvin Hopkins.

And the next few she things she found were what made her world standstill.

The more she dug, the more information she found that connected him to the person sending her those weird text messages several years ago and potentially sending them again as recently as the past few months. This man was in love with Philadelphia due in part because it was his home-town, but she could tell his passion for the City of Brotherly Love ran deep. There were at least twenty photos of the Hopkins' and the Wests' going on vacation together without the kids.

When she finally reached his contact information, her heart skipped a beat. The cell phone number that Calvin had listed in his profile area code was 215, which meant that at least at one point, he had a cell phone number with the same area code as the one that was texting Rae the vaguely threat-ening messages. She jumped up and grabbed a pen and paper and copied the number down from Calvin's profile, and then found the number that had sent her text messages from several years ago and the ones that started sending her messages recently.

Rae gasped and had to catch her phone because she almost dropped it. "You have got to be kidding me."

The numbers were almost the same; just the last digit was different.

What was she supposed to do with this information? She felt she could go to Jules, but didn't want to wake her in the middle of the night with circumstantial evidence. She could go to Flint, but that would also open up a whole can of worms regarding their relationship that she didn't want to deal with, even though she knew she had to at some point. She gathered the pen, paper, her phone, and a glass of water and tried to sleep on it even though she knew it would be almost impossible to do.

THE NEXT MORNING, she woke with a start. Based on the amount of sun shining into her room, Rae knew she had slept in.

She hopped out of bed and made her way into the living room, but no one was there. She turned around and hightailed it back toward the bedrooms and noticed that everyone's bedroom doors were open. Her friends had left their suite, and she didn't know where they went. Thinking they might have sent her a text message, she grabbed her phone and scanned her messages. She found one from Eve telling her that since she was sleeping, they grabbed breakfast, but they would bring her back some food and coffee.

Rae checked her other messages too and noticed that another day had gone by without Flint sending her anything. Although she understood if he had given up trying to talk to her, the thought of it still stung. She needed to figure out what she wanted to do with her love life and fast.

Looking around her room to find something to do, she figured the best course of action was to get ready in case the girls wanted to go shopping and exploring after she ate whatever they brought back.

As she was finishing putting on a light blue sundress, she heard voices outside of her door in the living room. She finished getting ready and headed out to meet her friends.

All the women greeted her with big smiles, and Eve handed

over the breakfast they grabbed for her. She scarfed down the food, not realizing how hungry she was, checked herself in the mirror once more, and asked, "So what's the plan for today?"

Liv answered, "We figured we'd take the bus to Hamilton and go shopping for souvenirs and see the sights down there if you didn't mind."

Rae nodded as she took the sunglasses she had placed on top of her head down and shielded her eyes with them. "I love that idea. I wanted to grab some jewelry for my mom anyway." And with that, off they went to explore more of Bermuda.

When they got back to the suite, the girls were exhausted.

"Do you mind if I take a nap before dinner?" Rae asked the room. She saw that the girls looked at one another before Jules responded, "That sounds like a great idea. I might do the same."

Rae raised an eyebrow at her. "Wow, you must be tired because I don't think you have ever mentioned taking naps in the time that I've known you."

"Guess we're rubbing off on her," Liv piped in as she placed the things she bought on the kitchen island. "How about you both nap and we'll wake you up before dinner?"

Rae and Jules both nodded and headed to their respective rooms. Rae set her souvenirs on top of her suitcase before sitting on her bed. She didn't even feel her head hit the pillow before she passed out.

RAE SLOWLY CAME to when she heard a knock on her door. She yawned as she stretched her arms above her head. The person on the other side of the door knocked again.

"I'm up. I'll be out in a few." Glancing out of the window, she noticed that the sun was setting, so she must have been sleeping for a few hours.

When she forced her body to get out of bed, she stretched all of her limbs. She left her room and immediately went into the bathroom to check the damage to her face and hair after that nap that turned into a mini sleep session. After thinking she looked presentable, she headed out of the bathroom before she realized something.

"Did I miss dinner? There's no way that it isn't after 5:00 p.m. now."

Feeling somewhat panicked, Rae opened the bathroom door and noticed, once again, that her friends' bedroom doors were all open too. Unless they were in the living room area, no one else was in the suite.

Shaking that thought from her mind, Rae grabbed her purse and left her bedroom. Thinking everyone might be in the living room waiting on her, she said, "Hey, ladies, I'm sorry about —" But the words died on her lips.

Her friends weren't in the living room. But someone else was.

She could see the outline of a man standing near the sliding glass doors leading out to their balcony. The man's attention was focused on the sun setting across the ocean from their balcony.

Her first thought was to run out of the room, screaming for help, but before her mind could process what she needed to do next, the man turned around.

"Flint?" Rae's shock quickly switched to anger. "What the hell are you doing here? A better question is, how the hell did you get here? Where are Liv, Jules, and Eve?"

"I'll answer your last two questions first as they're probably the easiest to start with. I took a plane to get here, and your friends are in the main lounge in the resort, probably enjoying a few cocktails and dinner on me."

"Is that how you bribed them to let you in here? Traitors." Her eyes were fixed on him while she paced the room to let some of her anger out. But she wasn't just angry at him. She would have to have a word with her so-called friends when she got done with Flint.

"I didn't bribe them."

"What did you do?"

"Begged and pleaded with them to give me a chance to explain myself to you. I found some new things out about what went down back home with us, my parents, and Cassandra. I also had to wrap some things up before I came here."

Rae's eyes never left Flint's as she tried to connect the dots. Yet she continued walking back and forth. "I think I also found some new information too."

Flint nodded. "That's great, I hope. But there are some things I want to say before we do a deep dive into that." Before he could continue, there was a knock on the front door of the suite. Flint checked his watch before heading to the door. "Right on time."

"Didn't know we were having a party," snapped Rae as she waited for him to reveal his latest surprise.

With his back to her, Rae took the time to admire him. She could tell that the white button-down shirt he was sporting was made of a linen material because she could make out almost every muscle that she assumed he was attempting to conceal under that shirt. And what a lousy job that shirt was doing of hiding anything. His light khakis and brown flip-flops made him look at home at this beach locale. Before he walked past her to the door, she noticed that his hair had a windswept look about it like he might have tried to style it, but gave up caring once he realized that the wind would have its way with it. Although she was pissed at him, she couldn't lie to herself and say that he didn't look great, especially given how he looked the last time she saw him.

Flint opened the door, and a man with a food cart entered the suite. He set up the food at the dining room table and a few minutes later was talking to Flint again before Flint walked him to the door. The suite's dining room table was now a dinner for two that included a beautiful Bermudan sunset.

"You seemed awfully sure that I would want to have dinner with you, huh?"

"I figured at the very least you would probably eat the dinner even if you didn't want to speak to me ever again. Food is life, as you would say."

Rae chuckled sarcastically but sat down at the dining room table. She saw Flint make a motion as if he would push her chair in, but she assumed he thought better of it. He quickly sat down in his seat. "I would ask if we could have a server in the room during dinner but figured it was a better idea for us to be alone while we talked."

Rae nodded. "So, let's talk." She told herself this would be over quick.

"Right." Flint cleared his throat and took a deep breath. "I want to start by saying that I love you. No matter what comes out of our conversation at dinner tonight. Also, whatever questions you have, I'll answer. I'm not holding anything back."

"I think I've heard that from you before." Rae didn't stop that snappy reply from leaving her lips, but instantly regretted it when she saw the look on Flint's face. "I'm sorry. I'll try to keep my snark to a minimum."

"I deserved it."

Rae shook her head and motioned him to continue as she ate a piece of the salad sitting in front of her.

"I'm sorry for everything that happened over the last couple of weeks. It shouldn't have even crossed my mind that acting like Cassandra and I were together was a viable option given that it would mean losing you and the relationship we had together. It was asinine, and I wasn't thinking straight."

Rae nodded her head, but her eyes never left her plate.

"So, I guess I should explain how I got here." He took another deep breath before continuing. "I vaguely remember you were talking about going to Bermuda with your friends, but I didn't make the connection when I knocked on your door a couple of days ago, and you didn't answer. I panicked and reached out to Jules because I didn't know who else to contact besides Danielle, which might have been weird."

"Yeah, I wouldn't have wanted to come back home to explain that."

Flint chuckled before continuing, "Yeah, wouldn't have wanted to do that on top of everything else that happened. So anyway, that's when I set my plan in motion to come to Bermuda to talk to you."

"How long have you been here?"

"Just a few hours. You don't want to know how much I

paid to make sure that I could get here. Not that it mattered to me anyway."

"Did Jules tell you where we were staying?"

Flint nodded his head.

"I should be mad at her, but I assume you told her something that convinced her it would be a good idea to tell you where we were on the island."

"Actually, I had to have a conference call with all of your friends together for them to reveal the location. Liv gave me the hardest time."

That caused Rae to smirk. That answer wasn't a surprise to her in the slightest.

"So, what did you tell them?" Rae pushed her salad aside and started on the steak dinner that was sitting to her right. She noticed that Flint had barely touched any of the food in front of him. "Are you not hungry?"

"I've been so distracted by trying to explain myself," he said before he took a bite of the salad before also pushing it to the side. Rae saw him practically salivating at the sight of the steak, so she hoped he would dig in. It would be a sin for any of this delicious food to go to waste.

"I explained to them that I thought this mess might involve my parents. Including back then and now." Rae could feel his eyes on her, but she didn't react.

"That makes sense, given how your mother was trying to throw Cassandra at you. How did you find that out?"

"My mom made a mistake and included me in an email that talked about how Operation Get Flint and Cassandra Together was going. The only issue was that everyone was bcc'd on the email, so I don't know who else she sent it to."

"What if I told you I think I know who was sending me

those text messages?" Flint's response was to cough. Rae realized she should have probably waited to drop that truth bomb until after he stopped drinking his wine.

"I think it was Cassandra's father."

"What made you think that?"

"Hold on." Rae jumped up out of her seat and hurried into her bedroom. She was back in record time, with the pen and notepad she had been using early this morning. "I hadn't had a chance to tell the girls about this today, but I was digging around on social media this morning and came across Cassandra's dad's social media information. Here is the cell phone number listed on one of his profiles, and here are the numbers that texted me."

"They're only a digit off."

"Exactly. Now, it's circumstantial, but I would almost bet my 401(k) that Cassandra's father is the one who has been doing all the weird things that have happened over the course of our dating."

"And I assume he would benefit if I were dating Cassandra."

"That's on top of them getting something out of the deal if you ran for Congress and won."

Rae looked at Flint after he didn't respond for a bit.

"This is all insane. Do you even want to run for Congress anymore?"

"I'm not sure. I want to continue to help the community the best I can, and I thought one of the best ways to do it was through running to represent the people I love. But I want to do it on my terms, and with the people I know will support me no matter what." Flint's stare into her eyes fixed her in place. "I love you, and I can't do this without you."

The air left Rae's lungs as she tried to catch her breath. "What are you trying to say?"

"I don't want to do this without you in my corner. My focus is on repairing things with you. And even if we get back together, if you don't want me to run, I won't. You mean too much to me for me to jeopardize this again."

"But isn't this your dream?"

"My dream is to be happy with you as long as you'll have me. That's what shook me to my core after you left. That's what also led me to snap out of even entertaining dating Cassandra for campaign funds. If this is something you want to do together, then we will do it. If you absolutely can't stand the intrusion it will have on our lives; then we won't. And if you want to send me packing and on my merry way, that's understandable too."

"You've given me a lot to think about, and I love you too."

Flint beamed. "I know. But I'm happy that you're at least thinking about it versus shoving me out the door on my ass."

Rae giggled as Flint grabbed her hand to play with it. "I missed that sound."

"What sound?"

"The sound of you laughing. The smiles you used to give me. I keep wanting to go back in time and change the past, but I can't. I'm so sorry, Rae."

Rae gently reached across the table and grabbed his hand. "It will be okay, no matter what happens. I promise."

27

"Brooke, could you let my father know I'm here?" Flint said as he walked up to the front desk of his father's office. Rae was trailing behind him, a little nervous about the stunt that Flint was about to pull. The couple had been back from Bermuda for about a week and had been laying low until this moment.

"He's in a meeting with your mother and the Hopkins'. Would you like to wait in the lobby until they're done?"

"Oh, what are the chances?" Flint shared a look with Rae. "I wanted to surprise them too. I'll just go in."

"I'm not sure if that's a good idea, Mr.—"

"Brooke, I'm Flint, remember. My dad is Mr. West." Flint gave her a charming smile before he walked around her desk and strolled down the hall to his father's office. He knocked on the door before entering. Rae decided that it might be best to hang back for the time being.

"The gang's all here. Hi, Dad, Mom. Mr. and Mrs. Hopkins."

"Flint? What are you doing here?" She wished she could

have seen the looks on their faces when Flint burst into the room.

"I'm here to stop whatever plans you're trying to cook up that involve me and Cassandra dating."

"I do not understand what you're talking about." Rae couldn't see Mr. West's face from where she was standing, but he sounded surprised.

"Wait, are you out of the loop? 'Cause I know for sure that Mom was involved in these shenanigans."

"Flint, we don't need to talk about this here." The worry in Gladys's voice was evident.

"But I think we do. Did you or didn't you tell me at a fundraiser a couple of weeks ago that I needed to date Cassandra to gain more financial support from potential future donors if I ran for Congress?"

"Fl—"

"Mom, please answer the question." Holding on to her purse strap a little too tightly, Rae took this moment to step into the doorway to watch everything unfold.

"Yes."

"Gladys, what? What's going on?"

"Oh, Terry, don't act so obtuse. You might not have been completely in on it, but you knew the deal. If Flint and Cassandra were to date seriously and get engaged to be married, we could have sold them as the new power couple. Could have been a hit locally or even nationally."

"But he's with Rae."

"And? The whole point of this was to make Flint see where his political and personal aspirations should be."

"Gladys, what the hell did you do?"

That led to Mr. and Mrs. West sniping at each other in front of the rest of the room. If Rae had to guess, this didn't happen often. Rae turned her attention to Flint and noticed that his face was slightly red as he clenched and unclenched his fists. She closed her eyes as she knew he would probably snap at any second.

"Enough!" Flint shouted. Rae somewhat hoped that Brooke had signed a nondisclosure agreement because she could probably make a lot of money selling this story to the press.

Flint looked at Calvin and Marie Hopkins before asking, "Were you both involved in this too?"

"What? Don't be preposterous. Marie and I would never—"

A shrill ringing of a phone stopped Calvin's speech in its tracks.

Rae approached from behind Flint with her head up high. "Whoever has been sending me text messages and stalking me is standing in this room right now. Why don't you answer the phone? I'm happy to redial the number if it goes to the automated voice mail." Although Rae was using general terms, her eyes were looking directly at Calvin. He finally dug into his pocket and clicked the ringer off.

"By the way, it's wonderful to see you again. We had only seen each other in passing on the metro, so it's lovely to see you up close and in person." The bitterness dripped from Rae's words, and her eyes were fixated on Calvin.

"What did you do, Calvin?" Gladys's high-pitched shout was aggravating to Rae's ears, but she refused to show that it affected her.

"You were taking too long to convince Flint that

Cassandra was who he should date, so I took matters into my own hands."

"Then why did the text messages start years ago?"

Gladys sat down in the chair that Rae assumed she had previously occupied. She looked winded, and Rae couldn't blame her, given the events surrounding her getting caught. "Long story short, we always imagined that Flint would run for Congress one day. It was something he always seemed interested in, and we encouraged it. When he joined the Air Force, it thrilled us he wanted to serve his country. Then he went to law school, helped start a nonprofit that he worked with on the side, and everything he was doing was fantastic with very few, if any, stumbling blocks. We were and still are proud of all of your achievements, Flint."

Gladys paused before continuing her side of things, "But along with that, we also knew that if the time came and you decided to further your political ambitions, this would all be good key points to reference in a campaign. Besides that, we thought you and Cassandra would get together when the time came, but we saw the way you looked at Rae even when you both first met. I knew she was more than likely going to be around for a while, and I knew that might shoot the plan we had to get you together with Cassandra in the foot. So we started trying to sabotage the relationship the first go-round. When you broke up, I knew that meant our plan was back on track, but I also understood that you were heartbroken, and I never wanted to see you in pain.

"When you came back home, the plan was to have you see Cassandra at random events that you were attending, given that you had mentioned that you had an interest in running for public office. Those 'random appearances' didn't do much because your mind and heart were focused on Rae." That was the first time that Gladys had looked at Rae since she had arrived. She couldn't read the feelings behind her eyes, but at least the look of disdain that she was used to wasn't there.

"Gladys, how could you—" Terry paused before looking at Calvin. He was leaning back on his desk; his knuckles had gone white from clutch the edge of his desk. "How could you both do this?" Terry's question led to a slew of answers from Gladys and Calvin.

Rae watched Flint while the other people in the group were talking. She could see a vein in his neck, pulsing much more than usual. He was pissed.

"Hey!" Flint's commanding voice stopped the chatter in the room. Rae was convinced that she hadn't seen him this angry before. "We're still trying to clear things up. Was Cassandra involved in any of this?" Flint spoke up for the first time in a while.

"Other than having a crush on you and coming to her mother and me for advice? No."

"I can't believe you would go as far as to blackmail us. My own mother."

Gladys's head perked up. "What are you talking about?"

"You didn't tell me if I didn't break up with Rae, you would release a salacious photo of us?"

If the confusion on Gladys's face wasn't genuine, she was a fantastic actress. The realization hit, and she turned to Calvin and Marie with her eyes wide open. "You tried to blackmail my son?"

"You told me to do whatever it took to make sure that his relationship with Rae was over. The private investigator that we hired found the photo, and that was our last-ditch attempt to end their relationship. And it worked."

The bile in Rae's throat rose to the surface. "But it was you that delivered those flowers to my office a few weeks ago. Not someone you hired."

"That's because we couldn't afford to hire anyone else," Marie spoke up for the first time and sucked all of the air out of the room.

"Marie—"

"Calvin, we've caused enough trouble as it is. Enough is enough. These two deserve the full truth." She turned her attention back to Flint and Rae. "The truth is, we're almost broke. If you won your campaign and got into Congress with Cassandra at your side, we stood to make millions just by being associated with you. And that was the drive that made us desperate. I'm sorry that this went on for as long as it did."

Rae surveyed the room. Terry's and Gladys's mouths were agape while Calvin's red patchy face was staring at his shoes. The only person looking at Rae was Marie, who had tears in her eyes. Flint nodded. "Well, I think that answers all the questions we had. We're going to leave now."

"Flint, wait—"

"Mom, just let us go. The fact that you went this far with your scheme is enough. You went as far as to meddle in my relationship twice and threaten the woman I love multiple times. I don't want to say something I might regret. Just leave it alone for now, okay?" Not waiting for a response, Flint turned around and gestured for Rae to walk in front of him. As she left the room with Flint's hand on the small of her back, she turned her head quickly to see Mrs. West wipe a tear from her face as she watched her son walk out of the room.

"Well, that wasn't intense or anything." Rae spared a glance at Flint as they both waved at Brooke and walked to the elevators with their heads held high.

"You're telling me." Flint's labored breathing gave away that the situation had affected him more than she realized. His anger hadn't dissipated like she thought it had earlier in the conversation.

"Do you want to talk about any of it when we get back to our apartments? Whose apartment are we going to anyway?"

"How about mine?" Flint asked as he looked down at her but kept walking to the elevator.

"Sure. But I don't have any of my clothes or other items at your apartment." The elevator doors opened as soon as Flint pushed the button, and he held them open for Rae as they both entered.

"Trust me; you won't be needing any."

"Hey, John," said Rae, smiling as she sat down at her usual table. "I brought a special guest with me tonight." She gestured to Flint, whose hand she was holding as she walked through the entrance to the Green Hat. It had been a couple more weeks since the showdown at Flint's father's office. The couple had been busy after that and had just found time to come to the Green Hat tonight.

"Hey, I'm John."

"Flint. It's nice to meet you."

"You look familiar. Have we met before?"

"I met Rae at this bar a few years ago." Rae felt her cheeks heat when Flint looked at her with a smile before turning his attention back to John.

"How's everything going, Rae? Surprised, you beat the other ladies here."

"Good. Can't complain. And you don't know how hard it was to get here early versus on time or late." Rae chuckled before she continued, "Can I ask for your help with something before the girls arrive?"

"Sure. What do you want to do?"

Rae smiled at Flint before she said, "Can we use your television?"

About twenty minutes later, one by one, Rae's friends arrived and hugged her. She could tell that they weren't expecting Flint to be there.

"How did you get here so early? Did you order us drinks? And you brought Flint? What has gotten into you? Are you sick?" Liv reached over and checked Rae's forehead before Rae batted her hand away.

"No. I'm fine," she laughed as she took a sip from her red wine. "But y'all might want to sit down and watch that TV. Thanks, John!" she said as she gave John a wink.

The lights in the bar lowered a bit, and a video started on the screen closest to the four friends sitting in their favorite bar. Flint felt around for Rae's hand before he grabbed it and gave it a gentle squeeze.

Rae watched as her friends' jaws almost hit the table the longer they watched the video. She tried to pry Liv's hand from around her wrist because the pressure was becoming too much.

"He's running?!" Liv exclaimed while Rae massaged her wrist, after finally removing Liv's tight grip from her wrist. "You're running?!" She jumped up and ran over and placed her hands on Flint's shoulders.

"And he put you in the announcement video?" Jules turned to Rae wide-eyed. "This is a big deal on multiple levels."

Rae nodded as she turned her attention to Eve. Until that point, Eve hadn't said a word, but she looked over at her friend with a sad smile on her face. "I know this is what he wants, but are you sure that you want to handle this?"

Taking a moment to compose her thoughts, Rae responded, "I know it will be difficult, and chances are they will pick our lives apart on some level." She stole a glance at Flint. "But this is something he truly believes in, and I believe in him and his dreams, so we both figured why not?"

"Then I'll help you both in any way I can."

"I will too," Jules and Liv said in unison.

"Jinx, you owe me a soda," Liv said as she nudged Jules. Jules shook her head and turned her attention back to the television.

Rae chuckled at them and turned to Flint. "We can do this."

Flint beamed at her and said, "I know we can."